Dedalus European Classics
General Editor: Timothy Lane

The Fables of Ivan Krylov

The Fables
of
Ivan Krylov

Translated from the Russian
& with an Introduction by
Stephen Pimenoff

Dedalus

ARTS COUNCIL ENGLAND
Supported using public funding by

Published in the UK by Dedalus Limited
24-26, St Judith's Lane, Sawtry, Cambs, PE28 5XE
email: info@dedalusbooks.com
www.dedalusbooks.com

ISBN printed book 978 1 910213 51 3
ISBN ebook 978 1 910213 55 1

Dedalus is distributed in the USA & Canada by SCB Distributors
15608 South New Century Drive, Gardena, CA 90248
email: info@scbdistributors.com   web: www.scbdistributors.com

Dedalus is distributed in Australia by Peribo Pty Ltd
58, Beaumont Road, Mount Kuring-gai, N.S.W. 2080
email: info@peribo.com.au

First published by Dedalus in 2017
Translation copyright © Stephen Pimenoff 2017

The right of Stephen Pimenoff to be identified as the translator of this work has been asserted by him in accordance with the Copyright, Designs and Patents Act, 1988.

Printed and bound in Great Britain by Clays Ltd, St Ives plc
Typeset by Marie Lane

This book is sold subject to the condition that it shall not, by way of trade or otherwise, be lent, resold, hired out or otherwise circulated without the publisher's prior consent in any form of binding or cover other than that in which it is published and without a similar condition including this condition being imposed on the subsequent purchaser.

A C.I.P. listing for this book is available on request.

The Author

Ivan Andreyevitch Krylov was born near St. Petersburg in 1769 into a poor family of the minor nobility. Krylov trained for the civil service, but from his early years nurtured literary ambitions. As a young man he wrote for satirical magazines and the theatre, but was constantly thwarted by the official censor. At the age of forty he published his first book of Fables, works written after the manner of Aesop and La Fontaine. They were an instant success, and were followed over the next 35 years by another eight books.

The Translator

Stephen Pimenoff was born in Montreal in 1948 of Russian and Estonian parents. He read English and Mathematics at McGill University, and has been a writer and mathematics teacher. As a freelance journalist he has published many articles in *The Daily Telegraph*, *The Guardian*, *The Times* and *The Independent*, as well as a wide variety of magazines ranging from *Homes and Gardens* to *Index on Censorship*.

His main interest is the study of Russian language, literature and history, and he is currently working on a translation of 19th century *Russian Fairy Tales* by Aleksandr Afanasyev.

Contents

Introduction   9

Book One: I-XXII	21
Book Two: I-XXIII	51
Book Three: I-XXI	82
Book Four: I-XX	112
Book Five: I-XXVI	135
Book Six: I-XXV	167
Book Seven: I-XXVII	195
Book Eight: I-XXIII	228
Book Nine: I-XI	253

Extras: I-VI   265

Introduction

Ivan Andreyevitch Krylov was a Russian literary figure of the late 18th – early 19th centuries, prominent in his time but today known only for a large number of fables which he wrote after the manner of Aesop and Jean de La Fontaine.

He was born into a poor family in Moscow in 1769. Though he received little formal education, he was a talented child and was determined from an early age to educate himself. He started working life as an office clerk, but from the beginning nurtured hopes of a literary career. He wrote several comic operas and numerous plays – all of which were unsuccessful – before turning to satirical journalism, a field more promising, indeed rich with opportunities considering the extent of official corruption in the Russia of his time.

The Tsarina Catherine II – known to history as Catherine the Great – had acceded to the throne in 1762. She had proved at first an enlightened ruler, drawn to the ideas of the French Encyclopaedists. She corresponded with Voltaire, eagerly read the works of Rousseau and Montesquieu, and welcomed Diderot to Russia. Her liberal inclinations led her to engage the Republican La Harpe as a tutor to her grandson Alexander (later Tsar Alexander I). But after the French Revolution, fearing the spread into Russia of what she saw as subversive and objectionable beliefs regarding liberty and equality, she radically changed her views. Several publications that Krylov was involved in fell foul of strict new censorship laws and were shut down.

Tsar Paul, who succeeded Catherine in 1796, proved even

Introduction

more repressive, and for the five years of his reign Krylov disappeared from the literary scene. Had Krylov died in 1801 he would today be completely unknown, even in Russia. As it is, he went on to become one of the best-loved figures in Russian literature.

With the accession of Alexander I, conditions became more favourable for writers. Krylov wrote two successful plays, and in 1805 began to translate the fables of La Fontaine. He very soon realised that he could write fables of his own that were pithier, sharper, and more relevant to Russian society, and his first collection was published in 1809. These at last were writings in which his full genius came to flower. They are elegantly written, and flavoured with apposite allusions to Classical mythology, a good deal of humour and considerable satire on the manifold weaknesses and failings of human beings, especially figures of authority.

Certainly there was in his native land no shortage of ideas for his fertile imagination. In all, nine books, comprising 204 fables, were published in his lifetime. Together, they mark a milestone in the Russian literary heritage.

In 1825, with the suppression of the Decembrist uprising and the accession of Tsar Nicholas, another period of repression set in. The thirty years of Nicholas' reign were a lamentable period of corruption, incompetence and suffocating convention.

Corruption had always been bad in Russia, but in the first half of the nineteenth century it grew steadily worse, to the point where, in the words of Constantin de Grunwald, a biographer of Nicholas, "it gained even the highest spheres of the government". (Gogol's play *The Government Inspector*, which is well known outside Russia, gives a vivid picture of this corruption.)

Introduction

In his book, *The Shadow of the Winter Palace*, Edward Crankshaw has this to say: "Throughout the length and breadth of Russia there were very few judges or officials who could not be bought, if not with crude bribes, then by the promise of favours to come from rich and influential landowners, or of easy promotion or threats of professional ruin for failing to cover up the misdeeds of superiors."

A provincial official, A. M. Unkovsky, said in 1859: "The whole of our administration is one vast system of malfeasance raised to the dignity of state government." (quoted by de Grunwald).

Censorship kept the public from discovering the worst abuses. And not just censorship: the two greatest poets, Pushkin and Lermontov, were both at times exiled for what were called "subversive verses". Nevertheless, ordinary people had a pretty good idea about what went on.

And to official corruption was added indolence and incompetence. Early on in his reign Nicholas showed great frustration with the bureaucracy, threatening in 1826 to prosecute provincial governors who were negligent in enforcing government orders.

One of Krylov's last fables, *The Grandee* (Book 9: XI), on this subject, was rejected by the official censor. But by then the author's fame was so great that the censor's decision was over-ruled by the Tsar himself. Indeed, it is said that privately Nicholas roared with laughter when he read *The Grandee*.

The Fables struck an immediate chord with the public, and as they came out Krylov's fame grew among people of all ages and from all strata of society. The royal family were said to be enthusiastic admirers of his work, while children in even humble homes grew up knowing many of the fables by heart. He was heaped with honours, given a generous pension and the rank of State Advisor, and awarded the sinecure of a position in the newly opened public library.

As he aged he developed a reputation for being a genial eccentric, slovenly in his habits and scruffy in his appearance. Some called him "the laziest man in Europe". He was also a glutton, who could dispose of mountains of food at a sitting. Anecdotes of his behaviour abound. At a dinner party once he was said to have eaten a dish of open-topped pies, three or four plates of fish soup, several chops, a plate of roast turkey and some "miscellaneous things". On returning home he ate a bowl of sauerkraut and a loaf of black bread.

He never married, though his cook's daughter Sasha was widely thought to be his.

After his death in 1844 his fame continued to grow: streets throughout the land were named after him, and numerous monuments were erected to his memory.

Although the Fables are written in the form of poems (which have rhythm and rhyme, but are of irregular metre), Krylov is not generally considered to be among the front rank of Russian poets. He is simply a very wise and shrewd observer of human nature who was forced, because of the censorship laws, to cast his observations in the form of fables. The poet Zhukovsky called these fables "poetic lessons of wisdom", while Pushkin called their author "a true people's poet". Some of his observations have passed into the language as maxims and proverbs.

Many of the fables are very funny, and like other great allegorical writings such as *A Pilgrim's Progress*, *Don Quixote*, *Animal Farm* or *The Lord of the Rings*, can be read on different levels, and enjoyed by all, from young children to the very old. They are not intended to arouse indignation, but amusement.

One abiding puzzle about Krylov's Fables is that they are,

Introduction

like their author, almost unknown among the English public. This may be because of the form in which they are cast. Russian poetry is more difficult to translate than that of some other languages, for example French, the grammar, syntax and vocabulary of which are closer to English. (English speakers are sometimes baffled by the esteem in which Russians hold Pushkin and Lermontov.)

Be that as it may, although many English people have read, or at least heard of, the fables of Aesop and La Fontaine, few – even those with a good general knowledge of literature – know anything about those of Krylov. This is a state of affairs I hope to remedy with this book. Krylov deserves a reputation equal to that of the other two fable writers.

In the Fables, Krylov pithily and astringently satirises the hypocrisy, nepotism, chicanery and venality of those in authority; the stupidity, incompetence and arrogance of officialdom and the bureaucracy; and the manifold weaknesses and failings of ordinary people: their fickleness, sycophancy, greed, selfishness, vanity, conceit, ingratitude... There is no failing that escapes the eye of this shrewd observer of humanity.

Although all seven of the deadly sins (except gluttony, for obvious reasons) loom large, not all the Fables are negative and critical. Many human qualities are praised and held up for emulation: selflessness, industry, loyalty, love, friendship, perseverence... Some of the Fables are no more than humorous glimpses of life and human nature, or snapshots of the bizarre preoccupations of fantasists, eccentrics, idealists and dreamers. Others offer wry, sardonic glimpses of life and human relationships and behaviour. Yet others offer wise advice on the conduct of life, or are what journalists call "cautionary tales": warnings about the consequences of ill-considered behaviour.

Introduction

A favourite device of Krylov's is to present a rivalry between a small, humble, unassuming creature – a hedgehog or bee or worm – and a powerful, arrogant, boastful one – a lion or eagle. Sometimes this contrast is between inanimate objects; for example, a great river and a little stream. The little creature or thing invariably gets the better of the bigger one. Sometimes the bigger one comes to a sticky end, but as in all morality tales he comes to realise the error of his ways. Retribution and justice figure largely in Krylov's vision, and a recurring theme is the concept of hubris leading to nemesis.

People sometimes talk of "the world of Shakespeare", and in the same way it is possible to talk of the world of Krylov, and what an astonishing world it is!

These are the people, creatures and objects which have speaking parts in the Fables. There are twenty-nine animals, ranging from the elephant and the bullock, to the mole and the mouse; there are eighteen species of bird, from the eagle to the swan to the siskin; four fish; and nine insects. There are nine species of plant life, from the oak tree to the cornflower, two spirits, eighteen mythological creatures, twenty-seven humans, from kings to beggars and knights to thieves, and twenty-three inanimate objects, from mountains to stones, and ponds to seas. And that is not even to mention the ones with just walk-on roles.

All these characters exhibit their own distinctive personality. The fox is scheming and crafty, the donkey is stupid, the wolf is dangerous, the lamb is innocent, the eagle is proud and majestic, the ox is honest but dull-witted, the ant is industrious, and so on.

Some of the Fables – thirty-seven, in fact, and mostly found in the first three books – are reworkings of those by either Aesop or La Fontaine, or both. But even those that Krylov adapted from earlier writers tend to be stamped with his own personality and brand of humour. Aesop's fables are for the most part very spare and to the point. Krylov developed and expanded them, and brought them to life by introducing local colour and detail; and he made them more vivid through the use of dialogue.

For some of his Fables, Krylov took a well-known saying or proverb and illustrated it by spinning it out into a tale: "As you sow, so shall you reap", or, "Shoemaker, stick to thy last", or, "A stitch in time saves nine". Other Fables are merely illustrations of maxims and folk sayings: "The leopard does not change its spots," or, "A poor workman blames his tools".

Solid, earthy common sense and a long acquaintance with the ways of the world lie at the root of Krylov's observations. Moreover, these observations are timeless: one has only to open a newspaper or turn on the television to see ordinary people as well as public figures who today display the very failings he writes about. It is a reminder, if one is needed, that human nature is unchanging.

A word on my translations themselves. Sometimes new translations of literary classics are described approvingly as being "modern"; that is, they employ current vogue expressions, as well as contemporary idiom and vocabulary, and catch phrases with only modern associations. I have avoided such language, feeling that as Krylov is not a contemporary writer, there is no reason why his works should read as if he is. Nowhere in the pages that follow will the reader find words, cliches or idiomatic constructions of recent coining, whether of British, Australian, American or other provenance, such as edgy, feisty, gutsy, fantabulous, no-brainer, brownie points, stitch-up, and thousands of others. Nor are there any modern, over-worked catch phrases like: to tick all the boxes, to step

Introduction

up to the plate, to throw in the towel, and so on. I felt that such ephemeral expressions with only modern associations would jar upon the reader's sense of fitness.

On the other hand, I have avoided also gratuitously using archaic language solely in an effort to add "period colour" by imparting a spurious old-world tone to the fables. Such a result would be as artificial as the other. Thus, I have used no words like mayhap, methinks, withall, sith, prithee, and so on, or expressions like "an I wist", "for the nonce" and "beshrew me". These English archaisms would be as much out of place in a translation of Krylov as would be many contemporary English expressions. In those places where Krylov has himself used an archaic or colloquial Russian word or expression, I have chosen the nearest English equivalent which, without being a modern coining, would be intelligible to modern readers. In short, I have tried to present a living picture of the era in which Krylov writes by using plain, intelligible English and without having recourse to any linguistic tricks.

I have not translated certain Russian words like *kasha*, *kaftan*, *borscht*, or *dacha*, even though they have rough English equivalents (gruel, tunic, vegetable soup and country-house); nor have I translated some words which have no precise English equivalent (*rouble*, *kopek*, *tsar*, *arshin*), as they are words found in any good English dictionary. This is because I wished to maintain the flavour of Russian-ness in the fables, and not have them read as if they had been written in English, or set in Yorkshire or the Australian outback. I have also translated literally certain expressions which would not normally be found in English writing. For example, when disaster befalls a Russian peasant he often says, "God visited me." This somewhat un-English sentiment conveys very well the uniquely Russian combination of resignation, fatalism and superstition which marks their religion and outlook on life generally, and I thought it worth preserving.

By the time Krylov was writing, in the first half of the 19th century, the modern Russian language was already well-established. It is true that the alphabet contained several unnecessary letters, which were eliminated after the Revolution, but the presence of these provides no serious obstacle to the understanding. A Russian person today reads Krylov as easily as a modern English person reads Jane Austen.

Though the lines of the Fables are of irregular metre, they do have a pleasing rhythm, and there is a strict rhyming pattern to most of them. Krylov had a great advantage in that Russian is a language well-suited to poetry. It is rich, expressive and beautiful, and is capable of great economy and conciseness. It is also a language in which it is easy to rhyme. (Lermontov once said in a letter to a friend that he felt it to be a stroke of great good fortune that their language was Russian, as he felt no other to be its equal.)

And so a conundrum I had to face was: what is the best form to put the Fables into? I rejected the idea of presenting them as prose, thinking that would make them lose their vigour, make them bland and sterile. I also dismissed the idea of maintaining the rhyming patterns. I felt that the necessity of choosing a less appropriate synonym for a particular word simply because it happened to rhyme would lead to a loss of accuracy and hence a straying from, if not an outright distortion of the author's meaning.

In the end, bearing in mind that it is not primarily as a poet, but rather as a satirist and social critic that Krylov is known, I decided to put the Fables into free verse. But I kept the format and structure of the originals, which explains why the lines are of different length. I felt that this would offer at least one of the advantages of modern poetry, chiefly more freedom to alter word order so as to preserve a satisfactory rhythm in the lines, without sacrificing precision of meaning. And although I have not padded out the lines unnecessarily, I have in places inserted a word that is not strictly necessary, so as not to produce too jarring a cadence. In short, I went as much as possible for sound as well as sense. So what has resulted are not adaptations, nor indeed literal translations, but what I call "faithful" translations.

I was very aware of the great danger to be guarded against in the translation of poetry. If a translator has no gift for the writing of poetry, but tries to reproduce both rhyme and metre, the result may prove to be just doggerel or, at best, verse of a lower quality than the original. This would give readers no indication of the greatness of the original, and would leave them questioning the high reputation of its author. One solution might be for a translator to collaborate with a recognised poet in the translation of a work. However, in that case the result would not strictly be a translation, but an adaptation. Those fables which Krylov adapted from Aesop should, if one is to be pedantic, be said to be by Krylov, "with acknowledgements to Aesop".

In the final analysis translations of poetry are always inadequate in one way or another: one simply has to choose the particular way in which one wishes to be inadequate. To derive the fullest all-round benefit from the Fables one would have to learn Russian and read them in the original.

Finally, where Krylov quotes peasant conversation, I have not, the way English writers sometimes do, used any regional or uneducated English dialect to indicate that the speaker comes from the lower stratum of society. Krylov's language is usually the purest Russian, even when he introduces colloquial

Introduction

expressions, so I have tried to render it into the purest, timeless English – English that would have been understood equally by Jane Austen (Krylov's contemporary) and a reader today. To what extent I have succeeded in this endeavour must be for others to judge.

I would like to thank Mrs. Masha Lees, a Russian scholar of great accomplishment, for reading over my translations and making many suggestions. But I did not always take her advice, and therefore must assume final responsibility for what follows.

Cheltenham, 2017

Book One

I
The Crow and the Fox

How many times has the world been told
That flattery is vile and harmful? But it has done no good:
In the heart the flatterer always finds a little corner.

God sent to a Crow somewhere a little piece of cheese.
Having settled herself on a fir tree,
The Crow prepared to breakfast.
She grew thoughtful, holding the cheese in her beak.
Unfortunately, a Fox happened to be running near;
The scent of the cheese stopped the Fox in her tracks:
She saw the cheese, and was captivated by it.
The cunning creature approached the tree on tiptoe.
Twitching her tail, and not taking her eyes off the Crow,
She said so sweetly, scarcely breathing:
"My dear, how beautiful you are:
What a neck you have, what wonderful eyes!
They are such as to be found only in fairy tales!
What feathers! What a nose!
And indeed, angelic must be your voice!
Sing, my dear, don't be shy! If, little sister,
With such beauty you are also good at singing,
Surely you would be our queen of birds!"

From flattery the Crow's head was turned,
With delight her breath was taken away;
And at the friendly Fox's words
She cawed with all her might.
The cheese fell – and was caught by the cunning Fox.

II
The Oak and the Reed

A thin Reed was once addressed by an Oak.
"Indeed, you have a right to grumble at nature.
To you, even a sparrow is heavy.
No sooner has a light breeze covered the water with ripples
Than you sway, begin to weaken,
And bend so like a suppliant
That it is a pity to look on you.
Whereas, on a level with the Caucasus,
Not only do I haughtily block out the rays of the sun,
But, laughing at whirlwinds and thunderstorms,
I stand firm and straight,
As if guarded by an inviolable world.
To you, all are storms – to me everything seems a zephyr.
If only you were growing in my vicinity,
Covered by the dense shade of my branches,
From bad weather I might be for you a defence;
But your destiny, allotted by nature, is to inhabit
The turbulent shore of Aeolian possession.
Plainly she does not care at all for you."
"You are very sympathetic," said the Reed in reply,
"But don't worry about me: I am spared many ills.
I do not myself fear whirlwinds;

Though indeed I bend, I do not break:
So storms damage me little;
Indeed, they threaten you much more.
It is true that until now their ferocity
Has not overcome your strength,
And from their blows you have not reeled;
But – let us see what happens!"
Hardly had the Reed said this
When suddenly, from the north, with hail and rain,
A tempest swept in with a roar.
The Oak stood firm: to the ground bent the little Reed.
The wind howled; it re-doubled its strength;
It raged – and tore away from the base
That one whose summit used to touch the sky,
And whose roots stretched to the underworld.

III

The Musicians

A man invited his neighbour to a meal.
The host's pretext was: he loved music,
And enticed the neighbour to his place to hear some singers.
The choir began to sing: out of tune and all at odds,
But with all the feeling they could summon.
The guest's ears ached from the cacophony,
And his head began to spin.
"Pardon me," he said with astonishment,
"What is there to admire here?
Your choir is just making a din!"
"That is true," replied the host with admiration.
"They do rather tend to bawl;

On the other hand, they take no alcohol,
And are all very well behaved."

But I say: it is better to drink,
And know what you are doing.

IV
The Crow and the Hen

When the Prince of Smolensk,
Craftily arming himself against invasion,
Placed a trap for a new wave of vandals,
And to their ruin left them Moscow,
Then all the inhabitants, both large and small,
Not wasting an hour, prepared to leave.
From the walls of Moscow they rose up,
Like a swarm of bees from a hive.
A Crow from a roof on all this alarming activity
Quietly, cleaning her beak, looked.
"And you, my friend, are you not going away?"
A Hen cried to her from a cart.
"Don't you know, they say that near the gates
Lies our enemy."
"What has that to do with me?"
Said the other to her in reply. "I shall stay here bravely.
You and your like can do as you wish;
But you know, they neither boil nor roast crows:
So I am bound to get on with the newcomers,
And may even succeed in profiting by
A piece of cheese, or a little bone, or something else.

Goodbye, crested one, pleasant journey!"
The Crow indeed remained;
But, instead of benefit from hoped-for scraps,
As the Prince of Smolensk began to starve the invaders,
She herself ended up in the pot.

Thus, often in calculations people are blind and foolish.
They seem to follow on the heels of fortune,
But the conclusion of the matter is:
They fall like the Crow into the pot.

V
The Casket

It sometimes happens to us
To think that labour and skill are needed,
Where we only have to guess
What simple course to take.

Someone acquired a Casket from a craftsman.
All noticed the perfection of the Casket's decoration,
And admired its beauty.
Then there entered the room a skilled mechanic.
Having examined the Casket, he said: "It has a secret.
Take a look; it does not in fact have a lock;
But I shall undertake to open it; yes, yes, I know I can;
Don't laugh up your sleeve like that!
I shall discover the secret, and shall open the Casket for you:
I am much admired in the mechanical arts."

So he set to work on the Casket:
He turned it from side to side,
And racked his brains;
Now he pressed a tack, then another one, then the clamp.
Watching him, others shook their heads;
They whispered, and laughed among themselves.
The only sounds they heard were:
"Not this way, that's wrong, not like that!"
The Mechanic laboured.
He sweated and sweated, and finally grew tired;
He gave up on the Casket.
He was at a complete loss as to how it opened.
But the Casket opened with a flick of the catch.

VI
The Frog and The Bullock

A Frog, having seen a Bullock in the meadow,
Was envious,
And undertook to become his equal in girth:
She started to pant, to puff herself up and swell out.
"Look at me, froggie," she said to a friend.
"Will I be his equal?" – "No, neighbour, far from it!"
"But look how wide now I swell;
So what about it?
Am I getting bigger?" – "Hardly at all."
"Well, how am I now?" – "Still the same."
She puffed and puffed, and the poor fool finished thus:
That, not having become as big as the Bullock,
She burst from the strain – and died.

Of such examples there are many in life.
Is it really surprising,
When the petty bourgeois want to live like their betters,
And small fry like nobles of distinction?

VII
The Choosy Maiden

A Maiden of marriageable age was thinking of a husband:
No blame in that;
Rather the blame lay in this: she was choosy.
She wished to find a bridegroom who was good, clever,
Highly decorated, honourable, and young
(The Beauty was very demanding);
Well, she wanted him to have everything –
but who has everything?
And note something else:
He had to love her, and not dare to be jealous.
Though it was strange, she happened to be lucky
That a selection of most noble suitors
Rolled up to her house.
But in her choice she had discriminating taste and ideas:
Such fiancés to other brides would have been treasures,
But at a glance she saw that
They were not fiancés, but mere excuses for fiancés!
How could she choose from among these suitors?
One was not high-ranking, another lacked decorations;
A third had rank, but, alas! empty pockets.
The nose of one was too wide, the eyebrows of another too thick;
Here was one thing, there was another;
Well, no one came who in any way represented her ideal.

The suitors stopped coming; two years passed;
Other suitors sent new matchmakers,
But they were suitors of only mediocre standards.
"What simpletons!" said the Beauty.
"Am I a bride for them?
Well, really, their practical jokes are out of place!
Even better suitors have I
Dismissed from the house with a bow.
How could I marry one of these nondescripts?
It is not as if I am in haste to marry;
To me the life of a maiden is not in the least burdensome:
During the day I amuse myself; and at night I sleep soundly;
Therefore it is not at all necessary for me to rush into marriage."
So this crowd of suitors also dispersed.
Then, hearing of these refusals,
Other suitors began to turn up more rarely.
A year passed – no one came;
One more year passed, a further whole year passed –
No one sent matchmakers to her.
So our Maiden grew into a mature young woman.
She began to compare herself to her friends
(And she had much leisure to compare):
One long ago had married, another was betrothed;
It was as if she had been forgotten.
Melancholy crept into the Beauty's heart.
When she looked into the mirror
It told her that each day evil time was stealing
Something of her charm.
First, the colour went from her cheeks; then the animation
from her eyes;
Appealing little dimples disappeared from her cheeks;
It was as if gaiety and playfulness had slipped away;

There, two or three little grey hairs peeped out:
Calamity all around!
Usually, without her, a gathering lacked sparkle;
Captive suitors crowded around her.
But now, oh! the old ladies invited her to play boston!
So now the conceited one changed her tune.
Reason ordered her to hasten into marriage:
She stopped putting on airs.
As a woman, she still looked coyly at men,
But her heart told her always the same.
So as not to finish her life in loneliness,
The Beauty, while she still had not entirely lost her bloom,
Entered into marriage with the first who asked.
And glad, very glad she was
To have married a cripple.

VIII
Parnassus

When from Greece the gods were expelled,
And their estates divided among dwellers of the earth,
Then even Parnassus was allocated to someone.
The new master began to graze donkeys on it.
The donkeys, I don't know how,
Knew that formerly the Muses had lived there,
And they said: "For good reason
Did they drive us to Parnassus:
Evidently the world had grown tired of the Muses,
And wanted us to sing here."
"Pay attention!" cried one. "And be of good cheer!
I shall strike up a song, and you join in.

Friends, don't be shy!
We shall bring glory to our herd,
And louder than the Nine Sisters
Shall we make music with our own choir!
But so that we make the position clear,
We shall establish this rule among us:
That those whose voice lacks a donkey's mellifluousness,
Will not be admitted to Parnassus."
The other asses approved of the donkey's
Fine and subtly-spun speech,
And a new choir of singers raised such a cacophony
That it seemed as if a convoy of carts had set out
In which there were a thousand unoiled wheels.
But how did the richly harmonised concert end?
The master, having lost patience,
Drove them all from Parnassus into the stable.

I would like, though not in anger,
To remind ignoramuses about a very old saying:
That if the head is empty
Then a change of scene will not serve to fill it.

IX
The Oracle

In a certain temple was a wooden god
Which began to deliver oracular utterances,
And to give wise advice.
For that reason, from head to foot,
It was covered in silver and gold,

And magnificently clothed in sumptuous attire.
It was laden with sacrifices, and overwhelmed with supplications,
And with incense over-perfumed.
In the Oracle all had blind faith.
Then, suddenly – oh horror, oh shame! –
The Oracle began to talk nonsense,
Began to give absurd and ridiculous replies;
And those who approached the Oracle, for whatever reason,
Simply heard it utter gibberish;
Well, all were astonished, and sought to discover
Whither had gone its prophetic gift.
But the explanation was that the idol was empty:
The priests had placed themselves in it
To prophesy to the local people. And so,
While there was a clever priest, the idol spoke intelligibly;
But when a fool sat in it,
The idol became a babbling idiot.

I have heard – have I not? – that in olden times
We saw such judges,
Who seemed very clever –
While they had a clever secretary.

X
The Cornflower

In the wilderness, a Cornflower that had blossomed
Suddenly grew sickly, shrank to almost half its size
And, bending head to stalk,

Despondently awaited its end;
Meanwhile, it plaintively whispered to the wind:
"Oh, if only day would come more quickly,
And the warm sun light up the field,
Maybe it would even revive me?"
"You really are simple, my friend!"
A beetle, rooting around nearby, said to him.
"Is it possible that the sun's only concern
Is to see that you grow,
And that he cares whether you fade or bloom?
Believe me, he has neither the time
Nor the desire for this.
If only you could fly, like me, and know the world
You would see that meadows, fields and orchards
Are only alive because of him, only flourish because of him:
He with his warmth heats vast oaks and cedars,
And richly confers astonishing beauty upon fragrant flowers;
Now those flowers are not at all like you:
They are of such value and beauty
That he pities them when they are cut down.
But you are neither luxuriant nor fragrant:
So do not torment the sun with your tiresome request!
Believe me, he will not cast a single ray on you,
So stop your futile yearning; be silent – and wither!"
But the sun rose, lit up nature,
And spread its rays in the Kingdom of Flora;
And the poor Cornflower, which had faded in the night,
With a look to the heavens revived.

Oh you, to whom high office was given by fate,
Emulate my sun!

Look: wherever his rays reach,
There he shows charity equally to a blade of grass and a cedar,
And spreads joy and happiness around himself;
Then his image shines in all hearts,
Like a bright ray in Eastern crystal,
And all pay homage to him.

XI
The Grove and the Fire

Choose your friends carefully.
When self-interest presents itself in the guise of friendship
It only sets a trap for you.
In order to understand this truth more clearly,
Listen to my little fable.

In winter a Fire smouldered under a Grove:
Perhaps it had been forgotten there by travellers.
With every passing hour the Fire became weaker;
There was no fresh wood: the Fire was barely burning
And, seeing its end, spoke thus to the Grove:
"Tell me, dear Grove,
Why is your fate so cruel,
That no leaf is to be seen on you,
And that you freeze entirely bare?"
"It is because I am covered in snow,"
The Grove replied to the Fire.
"In winter I can neither green up nor blossom."
"Nonsense!" continued the Fire to her.
"Just make friends with me; I shall help you;

I am brother to all suns, and even in winter time
Create marvels no less wondrous than the sun.
Ask in the greenhouses about fire:
In winter, when the snow lies thick and blizzards blow,
There, everything either flowers or ripens,
And it is all thanks to me.
Though it is not fitting to praise oneself,
And I do not like to boast,
Yet I by no means yield in strength to the sun.
Look, how here it arrogantly shines,
Then sets for the night without harm to the snow;
But around me, look how the snow melts.
So if you wish to green up in the winter,
As you do in spring and summer,
Give me a little place near you!"
So the matter was arranged: moving to the Grove,
The little Fire did not slumber, but grew to a blaze:
It ran through the twigs, through the branches;
And clouds of black smoke billowed to the sky.
All the Grove was engulfed in flames;
Everything perished utterly – and there, where on sultry days
Passers-by found refuge in the shade,
Stood only solitary scorched stumps.
But it was not surprising:
How can wood make friends with fire?

XII
The Siskin and Hedgehog

Loving solitude,
A timid Siskin at dawn twittered to himself:

Not because he wanted praise –
No, not at all for that – he just felt like singing!
Now, in splendour and all glory,
Phoebus, resplendent from the sea,
Arose.
It seemed that with himself he brought life to all
And on Candlemas Day, a choir of full-throated nightingales
Paid homage to him in the thick woods.
My Siskin fell silent.
"Why, friend," a Hedgehog asked him mockingly,
"Are you not singing?"
"It is because I do not have such a voice,"
The poor Siskin lamented,
"To honour Phoebus suitably in song;
And with a weak voice I dare not sing in praise of him."

―――――――

So too am I downcast, and regret
That the lyre of Pindar was not given to me,
Or I would sing praises to Alexander.

XIII
The Wolf and the Lamb

The strong always have the weak to blame:
Of that in history we have a multitude of examples.
But I do not write history;
So here is how it is shown in fables.

―――――――

A Lamb on a hot day went to a stream to drink;
But unfortunately it happened
That near that place was roaming a hungry Wolf.
He saw the Lamb and rushed towards the prey,
Though, to give his action a semblance of justification, cried:
"How dare you, insolent creature, with your dirty snout,
Stir up my clean water here with sand and silt?
For such impertinence I shall tear off your head."
"If his highness the Wolf will allow,
I beg to point out that I am drinking
A hundred paces downstream from his grace,
So there is no reason for him to be angry:
In no way can I be stirring up his drink."
"Therefore I lie!
Contemptible one! Was ever such impudence heard
in the world!
And I recall also that, the summer before last,
You were once rude to me right here;
I have not forgotten that, my friend!"
"Pardon," the Lamb replied, "But I am not yet even a year old."
"So it was your brother."
"I have no brothers." – "So it was a cousin or an in-law;
In a word, someone from your own family.
Your creatures, your dogs and your shepherds,
You all mean no good to me,
And always harm me if you can;
But I shall settle accounts with you for their sins."
"Oh, What am I guilty of!" – "Silence! I am tired of listening.
I have no time to analyse your guilt, you whelp!
You are guilty simply of this: that I happen to be hungry."
Thus he spoke, and to the dark forest dragged away the Lamb.

XIV
The Monkeys

When you imitate sensibly, then it is not surprising
If you derive benefit from it;
But if you imitate mindlessly,
Then – God preserve us – how bad it can be!
I shall take an example of this from a distant land.
Those who have seen monkeys know
How zealously they imitate everyone.
Thus, once in Africa, where there are many monkeys,
A whole tribe was sitting
On the boughs and branches of a thick tree,
And furtively looking at a hunter
As he rolled around in a net on the grass.
Each animal here quietly nudged his neighbour,
And all whispered one to another:
"Take a look at the daredevil;
There is really no end to his antics:
Now he goes head over heels, now he turns around,
Now, all in a ball, he so hunches up
That neither his arms nor his legs can be seen.
We really are adept at everything,
But such artistry have we never seen.
Beautiful companions!
It would be quite in order for us to imitate this man.
It seems he has amused himself enough;
Perhaps he will go away; then we, without delay…"
Lo and behold, the man indeed went off, leaving the nets behind.
"Well," they said, "do we have any time to lose?
Let's go and give them a try!"

The beauties came down. For these dear guests
A great number of nets had been spread out below.
They started to turn somersaults in them, to roll,
To muffle themselves up, to entwine themselves;
They shouted, they squealed; it was terrific fun!
But misfortune came
When they tried to extricate themselves from the nets.
The hunter meanwhile had been lying in wait,
And, seeing that it was time, approached his guests with crates.
They did their best to escape,
But not a single one was able to disentangle himself,
And the hunter easily captured them all.

XV
The Blue Tit

A Blue Tit set out from land:
She boasted
That she would burn up the sea.
The news spread immediately around the world.
Fear gripped the inhabitants of Neptune's capital;
Birds flew away in flocks;
And animals came running from the forests to see,
Not just whether, but how hot the ocean would burn.
And even, they say, having heard the rumours,
Those who love to partake in feasts
Were among the first to come to the shore with spoons,
In order to gulp down a fish soup of great richness,
Such as even the most generous tax-collector
Does not give to his secretaries.
They crowded: all marvelled in anticipation of the miracle;

They fell silent and, directing their gaze seawards, waited.
Only now and again someone whispered:
"Look, it's about to boil: look, in a moment it will catch fire!"
Nothing of the sort: the sea did not burn.
Was it boiling though? It was not even boiling.
And so how did the grand enterprise end?
The Tit flew off home in shame;
She became notorious,
But did not set fire to the sea.

To add to my words here it is appropriate to say
(Though not to single out anyone in particular),
That it is unwise to boast
Before bringing a matter to its conclusion.

XVI
The Donkey

When Jupiter inhabited the universe,
And was creating different species of creature,
Then the Ass too came into the world.
But whether from design,
Or preoccupation at such a busy time,
The fearsome god blundered,
And the Ass came out the size of a small squirrel.
Almost no one noticed the Ass,
Though in arrogance he yielded to no one.
The Ass would have liked to be held in esteem;
But how was that possible, having such size,
And ashamed even to be seen by the world?

The conceited Ass pestered Jupiter,
And began to ask for greater height.
"Pardon me," he said, "how is this to be endured?
Great honour is conferred on lions, snow leopards, elephants;
Everywhere, among both the great and the small,
All the talk is only about them, and them, and again them;
Why were you so unfair to the asses,
That you honoured them in no such way,
So that now nobody says a word about them?
If only I were the same height as a calf,
Then I would be a match for lions and leopards,
And the whole world would begin to talk about me."
That day, then again the next day,
My Ass pleaded to Zeus;
And pestered him to such an extent
That finally his entreaties were heard by the god,
And the Ass became an immensely great beast;
But more than that, he was given such a wild voice
That my big-eared Hercules
All but frightened away the other inhabitants of the forest.
"What sort of animal is that?" they asked. "Where does it come from?
Probably it has sharp teeth. And no end of horns."
And so everybody started talking only about the Ass.
But how did it all end? Hardly had a year passed
When all recognised the Ass' true nature:
The Ass for stupidity went into the proverb,
And now just carries water.

In rank and breeding it is good to be high-placed;
But what good is it when one's character is
found wanting?

XVII
The Monkey and the Spectacles

A Monkey towards old age suffered failing eyesight;
But from people she heard
That this was not such a great misfortune:
One only needed to acquire spectacles.
She got herself half-a-dozen pairs;
She turned the spectacles this way and that:
Now she pressed them to the top of her head,
Now she hooked them on her tail,
Now she sniffed them, now she licked them –
In no way did the glasses work.
"Foo-ee, to hell with it!" she said. "That one is a fool
Who listens to all those lies people tell:
Everything they told me about glasses is a lie;
There is not a bit of use in them."
The Monkey now, from vexation and grief,
Struck the spectacles so hard against a stone
That only fragments remained glittering in the light.

The same thing unfortunately happens with people:
However useful a thing is, not knowing the value of it,
An ignoramus rejects it for his own use;
And if the ignoramus is a little more advanced,
Then he even tries to destroy it.

XVIII
Two Doves

Two Doves lived together like brothers,
One neither eating nor drinking without the other.
Where you saw one, the other surely was there too;
Joy and sadness – all was shared between them.
They did not notice how the time flew by;
Sometimes they were sad, but never bored.
So: was it true that nothing was wanted,
Either by one friend or the other?
No: one of them bethought himself of travelling:
To fly, to see, to look over the wonders of the wide world,
To check lie against truth, to verify fact and rumour.
"Where are you going?" the other said to him mournfully.
"What use is it to roam about through the world?
Do you really wish to part from your friend?
Shameless one! If you do not pity me,
Then remember birds of prey, snares, terrible storms,
And everything else that makes travelling so dangerous.
At least wait for spring before flying so far;
I really shall not hold you back then.
But now food is still so scarce and poor;
And hark! The crow has just now raised a cry:
Surely this is a bad omen.
Stay at home, my friend.
We really are so happy together.
I do not understand, where in the world you still need to fly;
As for me, without you I shall feel orphaned.
Snares and kites and thunder will appear to me in sleep;
I shall start to fear that all misfortunes have befallen you:
Scarcely will even a little cloud have appeared overhead,

When I shall say: oh! where is my brother?
Is he healthy, does he have enough to eat, is he protected
from bad weather?"
This speech moved the other Dove;
He felt sorry for his brother, but the desire to fly was great:
It robbed him of both reason and sympathy.
"Don't cry, my dear," he said to comfort the other.
"For three days, not more, shall I be parted from you.
I shall briefly notice everything in flight on the way,
And, having viewed all the wonders of the world,
I shall return to the protection of my friend.
Then we shall have something to talk about.
I shall remember every moment and each place;
I shall relate everything: what goes on and what customs
are practised,
What wonders I see and where I see them.
You, listening to me, shall imagine everything so vividly,
As if you yourself had flown with me through the world."
Now – there was nothing else to do – the friends kissed,
Said goodbye and parted.
So our wanderer flew; suddenly, he encountered
rain and thunder;
Under him, like an ocean, the steppe around glimmered blue.
Where could he take refuge? Fortunately a dry oak
caught his eye;
Somehow our dove nestled inside, snuggled up in it;
But he was able neither to get protection from the wind,
Nor to hide from the rain: he was drenched
and chilled to the marrow.
The thunder abated a little. Hardly had the sun come out
When the desire of the poor thing to fly returned.
He shook himself and flew off – he flew, and saw:

On the ground under the wood were scattered grains of wheat.
He descended – and straightaway fell into a net.
Calamity all around!
He trembled, strained, struggled;
Fortunately, the net was old: somehow he tore it;
Only, he dislocated a leg and slightly crushed a wing.
But he paid no attention, and flew away regardless.
Now, to add to this misfortune, there was danger overhead:
Out of nowhere appeared an evil hawk;
Everything went black before the Dove's eyes;
With his last strength he fluttered his wings to try and escape.
But he was completely exhausted, and had not the strength.
Rapacious claws were already spreading over him,
And he felt a cold draught from the vast wings.
Then an eagle, directing its flight from the sky,
Struck the hawk with all its strength –
And a predator got the predator for dinner.
Meanwhile, our Dove,
Who had fallen like a stone, pressed himself under a wattle fence.
But his troubles had not yet ended:
One disaster always brings another.
A child, aiming at him a fragment of broken crockery
(This age does not know pity),
Threw it, and cut open the poor thing's temple.
Then our wanderer, with a cut head,
With a damaged wing, with a dislocated leg,
Cursing his desire to see the world,
Somehow arrived home without new mishaps.
Yet he was lucky: there, friendship awaited him.
To his joy, he found help in the care of a ministering spirit;
And with it he soon forgot all griefs and misfortunes.

Oh, you! who burn with the desire to travel the world!
Read this fable.
Whatever your imagination promises you,
Do not impulsively set out on such a distant journey.
Believe me: on this earth you will not find a better place
Than that where lives your friend or loved-one.

XIX
The Gold Coin

Is education useful?
Yes: no question about it.
But what we call education is often no more than
The sheen of sophistication and even the corruption of nature.
So one must be very careful
That when one strips from people the bark of roughness,
One does not also remove their good qualities,
And does not weaken their spirit, or spoil their basic nature,
Or separate them from their simple qualities
And, having given them only a useless gloss,
Bring to them mockery instead of acclaim.
Observations about this sacred truth
Could fill a whole book with grandiloquent language;
But not everyone should speak grandiloquently:
So, half in jest,
I intend to demonstrate this truth to you in a fable.

A peasant, of which there are everywhere not a few,
Found a gold coin on the ground.

The coin was dirty and caked in dust;
However, three handfuls of five-*kopek* pieces
Were offered to the peasant in exchange for the coin.
"Wait a moment," he thought, "I should be able to get
twice as much;
I have thought of something
That will make people more eager to buy it."
So, having taken sand, gravel and chalk, and having
obtained bricks,
My peasant set to work.
With all his might he ground the coin against the brick,
And rubbed it with gravel, and with sand and chalk;
Well, in a word, he wanted to make it shine like a flame.
And indeed, like a flame the coin began to shine;
But it became much lighter,
And lost its former value.

XX
The Trigamist

A certain sinner,
With a wife still living, married two more.
Now a rumour about this reached the Tsar
(And the Tsar was strict and disinclined to indulge such
behaviour).
He in an instant ordered the prosecution of the polygamist,
And the devising of such a punishment for him
That would leave the people in fear,
So that no one in the future would dare to commit
So great a crime.
"And if I see," he said, "that the punishment for him is too mild,

I shall immediately hang all the judges around the table."
To the judges this was bad news.
Fear threw them into a cold sweat.
For three days and nights they considered
What punishment they could devise for this criminal.
Thousands were possible; but from experience they knew
That, after all, people are not cured of such wickedness.
However, in the end God advised them.
The criminal was summoned for the announcement
Of the court's decision.
In a unanimous judgment,
They sentenced as follows: to let him keep all three wives.
The people were amazed at such a judgment,
And expected the Tsar to condemn all the judges to hang.
But not four days had passed
Before the Trigamist hanged himself;
And this outcome caused such fear
That since that time, to three wives,
No one in that kingdom dared to marry himself.

XXI
The Atheists

In ancient times there was a people, to the shame
of earthly tribes,
Who became embittered in their hearts to such a degree
That they armed themselves against the gods.
Rebellious crowds, behind thousands of banners,
Some with bows, others with slings, rushed to the battlefield.
The ringleaders among the hotheads,
To imbue the people with more of the fighting spirit,

Shouted that the court of heaven was too strict and senseless,
That the gods either slept or ruled foolishly,
And that without more ado it was time to teach them a lesson.
They pointed out, furthermore, that from the neighbouring mountains
It would not be difficult to hurl stones at the gods in the sky,
And to sweep Olympia with arrows.
Being embarrassed by the impertinence and abuse of these madmen,
All Olympia directed entreaties to Zeus,
To do something to avert catastrophe.
All the gods entertained the same thought,
That for the enlightenment of the rebels it would do no harm
To produce for example some little miracle:
To send either a flood, or a rumble of thunder,
Or even to strike them with a rain of stones.
"Let us wait," said Zeus, "and if, not fearing immortals,
They do not submit, and cease their unruly conduct,
They will punish themselves for their deeds."
Now, from the god-rebellious forces there flew up noisily into the sky
A multitude of stones, a cloud of arrows.
But, with thousands of deaths, cruel though inevitable,
The salvo rained down on their own heads.

———————

The fruits of such unbelief are terrible;
And know this, you people,
That the arrogant, blasphemous talk of self-proclaimed sages,
Who arm you against the Deity,
Simply brings nearer your fatal hour,
When all will turn into a rain of arrows against you.

XXII
The Eagle and the Hens

Desiring to gaze to his heart's content at the bright day,
An Eagle flew high toward the heavens,
And soared there in sheer delight,
Where lightning is born.
Having descended at last from the dizzy heights,
The king of birds sat to rest on a barn.
Though this is an unenviable perch for an eagle,
The King had his whims:
Perhaps he wanted to honour the barn,
Or perhaps there was nothing nearer to sit on more suitable to his rank,
Neither an oak, nor a granite crag.
I do not know what the intention was, only that the Eagle
Sat for a little while,
And straightaway flew over to another barn.
Having seen him, a crested brood-hen
Nudged her companion:
"Why are eagles held in such esteem?
Is it really for their flight, dear neighbour?
Well, really, if I wish,
Even I can fly from barn to barn.
We should really in the future not be such fools
As to consider eagles more noble than us.
They have no more legs and eyes than we do,
And you have just now seen
That they fly as low as hens."
Being sick of this nonsense, the Eagle replied:

"You are right, but not entirely;
An eagle can descend just as low as a hen,
But a hen can never rise to the heights."

When you judge the talented,
Do not spend labour in vain considering their weaknesses;
But, recognising what is strong and admirable in them,
Try to understand their different virtues.

Book Two

I
The Frogs Who Asked for a Tsar

The Frogs grew to dislike their national government;
But it seemed to them entirely wrong
To live without purpose and without a master to serve.
In order to assuage their grief,
They appealed to the gods to send them a tsar.
To listen to any nonsense would not be in the nature of gods;
Just this once, however, Zeus heeded them:
He gave them a Tsar. This Tsar flew noisily to them from the sky,
And burst into the kingdom so heavily
That the marshy state was shaken to its core.
In haste, in fright, the Frogs rushed away,
However and wherever they could,
And, whispering in their holes, gazed in awe at the Tsar.
And, indeed, it was a wondrous Tsar that had been given them:
Not a busybody, not a frivolous being;
Staid, taciturn and dignified:
Well-built and of great height.
Well, he was a wonder to behold.
Just one thing about the Tsar was unfortunate:
He was an aspen log.
At first, honouring his very high state,
None of his subjects dared approach him,
Looking on him with fear, and even then furtively,
From afar, through the sweet flag and sedge.

But as in the world there is no miracle
To which the world does not grow accustomed,
Then even they soon recovered from the fear,
And dared to creep up to the Tsar with devotion:
At first, they prostrated themselves before him;
By and by, those who were bolder tried to sit next to him;
Before long, those who were yet more bold
Were even sitting with their backs to the Tsar.
The Tsar tolerated it all with good grace.
A little later, anyone who wanted could even jump on him.
In three days life became boring with such a Tsar.
The Frogs presented a new petition,
That Jupiter give their swampy land a really good Tsar.
Granting their ardent request,
Jupiter sent to them in their kingdom a crane.
This Tsar was not a log, but a being of entirely different nature.
He did not believe in spoiling his subjects;
He ate the guilty; and in his court no one had any rights.
As a result, whether it was breakfast, dinner or supper,
The punishment was harsh for the inhabitants of the swamp.
It was a black year.
Each day saw a decline in the population.
From morning till night their Tsar stalked the kingdom,
And all whom he met,
He immediately condemned and – swallowed.
So, even more than before, did the Frogs croak and groan
In appealing to Jupiter to send them a different Tsar.
They complained that their Tsar swallowed them like flies;
That they could not even (how frightful this was!)
Either show their faces, or croak safely;
And that, in a word, their Tsar was more unbearable
than a drought.

"Why on earth," thundered a voice to them from the sky,
"Were you unable to live happily before?
Am I to have no peace from you, mad ones?
Did you not keep pestering me to grant you a Tsar?
So a Tsar was given to you – that one was too quiet;
You rebelled in your pond;
Another was given to you – that one was the soul of evil:
Now live with him, so that it may not be even worse for you."

II
The Lion and the Snow Leopard

Once, in olden times, a Lion
Was engaged in a very long-running dispute with a
Snow leopard
Over disputed forests, over thickets, over dens.
Neither had the ability to determine his rights according to law.
Of course, the strong are often blind to the law:
In these matters they have their own rules:
Whoever dominates, that one is right.
But in the end, so as not to be forever fighting –
And simply blunting their claws –
Our heroes decided to investigate their rights,
And look into ways of ceasing hostilities:
To end all discords,
And then, as usually happens, to declare perpetual peace –
Until the next quarrel.
"Let us both quickly appoint for ourselves representatives,"
The Leopard suggested to the Lion,
"And what they decide, so even let it be.
I, for example, for this shall choose a cat:

Though the little beast be unprepossessing, its conscience
is clear;
And you appoint an ass: it really is a most noble animal
And, I may say, it is by far the most enviable of your beasts.
Believe me, as a friend, all your advisors and courtiers
Are hardly worth his little hoof.
Let's agree to accept the judgment
That he with my little cat will deliver."
The Lion agreed without argument to the Leopard's proposal;
But he appointed, not an ass, but a fox
To represent himself in the dispute,
Having said to himself (as he evidently knew the world):
"In that one whom the enemy praises, there is really no use."

III
The Grandee and the Philosopher

A Grandee, talking with a Sage in an idle hour
About this and that, said,
"Tell me, you know the world well enough,
And you read in the hearts of people as if in a book:
How is it that whatever we set up –
Whether we establish courts or learned societies –
We have barely averted our eyes
Before the first boors worm their way in.
Can it be that there is no remedy at all against them?"
"I think not," said the Sage in reply.
"Societies suffer the same fate (between ourselves),
As do wooden houses."
"What do you mean?"
"Just this: I recently finished building my house.

We have not yet settled in,
But already the first termites have made their appearance."

IV
The Animal Plague

The most cruel scourge of the heavens,
terror of nature – plague –
Rages in the forest. The animals are in despair;
The doors to hell swing wide open:
Death roams the fields, the valleys, the mountain tops;
Everywhere are scattered victims of its ferocity;
Inexorably, like hay, it mows them down.
And those who are alive,
Seeing death at hand, wander around barely living:
Fear has utterly transformed them.
They are the same animals, but not engaged
in the usual practices.
The wolf does not kill the sheep, and is as submissive as a monk;
Having given peace to the hens, the fox fasts in his earth:
He does not even think about food.
The turtle-dove lives apart from his mate,
Of love there is no more thought.
But without love, what joy can there be?
Amid this grief the lion summoned the animals to a council.
They dragged themselves along step by step, barely holding
on to their souls.
They trudged along together and, in silence,
sitting around the tsar,
Fixed their eyes and applied their ears.
"Oh, friends!" began the lion, "For a multitude of sins

Have we incurred the terrible anger of the gods.
So, let that one among us who of all is most guilty –
Let him of his own free will
Offer himself as a sacrifice to them!
It may be that in this way we shall please the gods,
And that the sincere ardour of our belief
Will assuage the intensity of their anger.
Who among us, my friends, does not know
That there have been in history
Many examples of such voluntary sacrifice?
Thus, in a spirit of submission,
Let us confess here, all of us, aloud,
Where and when we have sinned, wittingly or unwittingly.
Let us confess, my friends!
Ah! I shall confess – even though it pains me –
That even I am not innocent!
The poor little sheep – and for what? – they were
entirely guiltless.
I killed them cruelly,
And sometimes – who is without sin? –
It happened that I even killed a shepherd;
And so I readily give myself up for sacrifice.
But it would be better first for all of us, one by one,
To detail our sins: whoever has most of them,
That one should be sacrificed:
This is what would be most pleasing to the gods."
"Oh, Tsar of ours, kind Tsar!" said a fox,
From excessive goodness you consider your acts to be sins.
But if we all start to listen to the timid voice of conscience,
Then in the end we shall all die of hunger.
And besides, father of ours,
Believe me, it is a great honour for sheep

When you are good enough to eat them.
As for shepherds, we all here offer humble thanks to you.
It serves them right: we must teach them a lesson more often.
That tailless race just behaves with stupid arrogance,
And everywhere lords it over us."
Thus concluded the fox. After her, in the same way,
The other flatterers said the same to the lion.
Vying with one another, all hurried to show
That there was no reason for the lion to ask forgiveness.
After the lion, the bear, and tiger, and wolf, in their turn,
Humbly confessed their sins to all.
But no one dared to look too deeply into their godless doings,
And all who were there were well-endowed,
Either with claws, or with teeth – those were seen to be,
By everyone, not only right, but almost saintly.
In his turn, the humble ox now mooed to the gathering:
"I too have sinned. Five years ago,
When in winter food for us was scarce,
The devil directed me to sin:
Not having been able to find food anywhere,
From the priest's rick I stole a morsel of hay."
At these words a clamour arose;
Bears, tigers, wolves shouted:
"Oh, what a scoundrel!
To eat someone else's hay! Well, is it a wonder
That because of his lawlessness the gods are so angry at us?
Him, obnoxious beast with head horns,
Bring him to the gods for all his mischief,
In order to save our souls from contagion.
It is because of his sins that we have such a plague!"
They approved the condemnation –
And lifted the bull on to the bonfire.

Of people too, in the same way, they say:
He who is most submissive, even that one is deemed guilty.

V
Canine Friendship

Beneath the kitchen window, in the sun,
Polkan and Barboss were lying down warming themselves,
Although it would have been better if they had been
By the gate at the front, guarding the house;
But as they had already eaten quite a lot –
And besides, were most courteous dogs,
And barked at no one during the day –
So the two of them began to talk
About all sorts of things: about their canine duty,
About evil, about good, and finally about friendship.
"What can be more agreeable," said Polkan,
"Than to live in close intimacy with a friend;
To support each other in everything;
To sleep and to eat with a friend,
To stand like a rock behind the friendly fur
And, finally, to gaze in one another's eyes
In order to share the happy moments;
If possible to amuse and entertain each other a little,
And to derive all one's bliss from mutual happiness!
So if only, for example, you and I
Were to have such a friendship,
I should say with confidence
That we would not see how the time flies."

"But what is to be done?" replied Barboss.
"That's the way it is!
For a long time, dear Polkan, it has pained me,
That, though we are dogs of the same house,
We do not live a day without a fight;
And why? Thanks to the master,
We are neither hungry nor confined.
Besides that, really, it is a shame
That although the dog since ancient times
Has by Man been held up as an example of friendship,
Friendship between dogs, like that between people,
Is almost entirely unknown."
"We shall give an example of it in our time," cried Polkan.
"Give me your paw!" – "Here it is!"
And the new friends began to hug;
They began to kiss;
They knew not, in their joy, to whom to compare themselves:
"My Orestes!" – "My Pylades! Away with fights, envy, malice!"
Here, the cook unfortunately threw a bone from the kitchen.
The new friends raced each other to it.
What happened to the harmony and concord?
My Pylades and Orestes started to fight;
Tufts of fur flew upwards:
In the end they had to be drenched with water.

The world is full of such friendship.
About friends nowadays one can say, without sinning,
That in friendship they are nearly all alike:
To listen to them it seems they are soul-mates;
But just throw them a bone and they behave like your dogs!

VI
The Reckoning

Sharing a common house and a common office,
Some worthy tradesmen made a pile of money;
They finished trading and showed a profit.
But when are spoils divided without argument?
They began to shout: about the money, about the goods,
When suddenly a cry went up that their house was on fire.
"Quickly! quickly!" shouts one, "save the goods
and the house!"
Another shouts: "Let's get out first, and settle accounts later!"
"But first pay me my thousand," shouts a third,
"I'm not leaving until you do."
"I am two thousand short," one more shouts.
"The accounts are clear about that,"
"No, no, we don't agree!"
And so went the hows and whats and whys…
Having forgotten that the house was on fire,
The mischief-makers here made a fuss
To the point where they were enveloped by the flames;
And all perished along with their possessions.

———————

From matters that are far more important,
Quite often ruin comes to all.
Instead of meeting common misfortune together,
Each starts an argument
About his own concerns.

VII
The Barrel

A man asked his friend
To lend him his barrel for about three days.
To do a favour for a friend is a sacred thing!
Of course, if the request were for money it would be different:
There, friendship is put aside, and one could refuse;
But why not lend a barrel?
When it was returned
It was again used to carry water.
All would have been well, except for this:
The barrel had been borrowed by a tax-collector,
And had stood for two days full of wine,
So that from it the scent of wine had gone into everything:
Whether *kvas*, or beer – why, even into food.
For nearly a year the owner struggled with it:
Now he steamed it, then he left it in the fresh air;
But whatever he put into that barrel
Was left with the scent of wine;
And with the barrel at last he was compelled to part.

Try not to forget, friends, this fable:
To harmful studies in youthful days
You have only to be exposed once;
After that they will influence you all your life,
No matter what you say
And no matter what you do.

VIII
The Wolf in the Kennel

A Wolf at night, thinking to get into the sheep-fold,
Got into the kennel.
The whole yard sprang suddenly to life.
Scenting the grey trouble-maker so near,
And spoiling for a fight, the dogs began to bark.
The houndsmen shouted: "Alas, lads, a thief!"
And in an instant the gate was locked;
In a moment the kennel became bedlam.
Men came running: one with a cudgel,
Another with a rifle.
"Light!" they shouted. "Light!" They came with torches.
My Wolf sat, having nestled up with his back in the corner.
Teeth snapping and fur bristling,
He showed with his eyes that he wanted to eat everyone;
But, realising that he was not here confronting sheep,
And that now, at last, had come
The moment of reckoning for his past,
The sly creature began to negotiate,
And began thus: "Friends! Why all this commotion?
I, your old kith and kin,
Have come to make peace with you, not at all to quarrel;
Let's forget the past, let's establish general good will!
Henceforth, not only will I not worry the local sheep,
But will myself be glad to fight others in their defence,
And I assert with a wolfish vow that I…"
"Listen, neighbour,"
The head houndsman here interrupted,
"You are grey-haired by nature, but I am grey-haired with age:
For a long time have I known your wolfish nature;

And that is why it is my custom
Not to make peace with a wolf –
Until I have taken off his skin."
And he straightaway released the pack of hounds on the Wolf.

IX
The Stream

A shepherd by a little Stream sang mournfully in sorrow,
About his misfortune and his irrecoverable loss:
His beloved lamb
Not long before had drowned in the river.
Hearing the shepherd, the Stream murmured angrily:
"Insatiable river! If your waters
Were such as mine,
Both clear and shallow,
Then everyone would see in their depths
All the victims whom you have so greedily devoured.
It must be from shame that you gouged a channel
in the ground,
So as in dark abysses to hide yourself.
I believe that if to me
Fate had given such abundant waters
I would have become an ornament of nature,
And would not do harm to so much as a hen;
How carefully would my water flow,
Past huts and every little bush!
The banks would only bless me.
I would refresh valleys and meadows,
But from them would not take away a leaf.

Well, in a word, in my way I would do good.
Not causing anywhere either trouble or grief,
My water, to the sea,
Would flow as pure as silver."
Thus spake the Stream, thus indeed it thought.
But what happened? Not a week passed,
Before a storm-cloud settled itself over a mountain nearby.
With the riches of the rain water the Stream suddenly became a river;
But, oh! whither had gone its humility!
Against the shores it beat with turbid flow,
It seethed, roared, whirled dirty foam in thick masses,
Dragged hundred-year old oaks;
In the distance was heard only the sound of loud cracking.
And the very same shepherd, on whose behalf the Stream
Had not long before so eloquently berated the river,
Perished in it with all his flock;
And traces even of his hut were swept away.

How many little streams flow so quietly, smoothly,
And murmur so sweetly to the heart,
Only because there is little water in them!

X
The Fox and the Marmot

"So whither, my friend, are you running so fast?"
A Marmot asked a Fox.
"Oh, my dear friend!
I have been slandered, and was exiled for bribery.

You know, I was a judge in the hen-house,
And lost in the duties both health and peace;
Because of my work I was unable to feed on even a scrap;
At night I was not getting enough sleep;
And because of that I fell under suspicion;
And it was all due to slanders. Well, you yourself think:
Who on earth would be innocent if the world listened to slanders?
Would I take bribes? I really would be mad to do so!
Well, did you ever see – and I shall quote you –
That I was guilty of this sin?
Think, try to remember."
"No, my friend; but I quite often saw
That you had your snout in the down."

Somebody, some place, sighs so heavily,
Saying he is living on the last *rouble*:
And indeed, all the town knows
That he has money neither for himself
Nor for his wife.
But then you notice that little by little
He first builds a house, then buys the village.
And when you compare his income with his expenditure,
You will not sin if you say
(Though in court you cannot prove it)
That he has feathers in his snout.

XI
The Passers-by and the Dogs

Two friends were walking one evening,
And conversing agreeably between themselves,

When suddenly from a gateway
A mongrel yapped at them;
After it, another; then two or three more, and in an instant
From all the yards some fifty dogs came running.
One of the walkers had already seized a stone
When the other said to him: "Hold off, brother!
You will not stop the dogs from barking,
You will only tease the pack more;
Let's go on: I know their nature better than you."
And indeed, they had walked barely fifty steps
When little by little the dogs began to quieten down,
Until at last their barking was heard no more.

Envious people, looking at anything,
Always raise a clamour;
But continue on in your own way:
They will shout and finally lose interest.

XII
The Dragonfly and the Ant

A frivolous Dragonfly
All the beautiful summer sang;
She had no time to notice
How quickly winter came.
The open field froze over;
No more came those bright days
When under each leaf
Shelter and a meal awaited her.
Everything vanished: with the cold winter

Need and hunger set in;
The Dragonfly no longer sang:
To whom indeed does it occur
To sing on an empty stomach?
Overcome with deep melancholy,
She crawled to an Ant:
"Don't abandon me, dear neighbour!
Let me regain my strength,
And just until spring-time
Feed and warm me!"
"Dear friend, it is strange to me,"
The Ant said to her.
"Did you not work in the summer?"
"How could I have had time, dear?
Lying in the soft grass I had
A life full of songs and games,
Enough to make the head spin."
"And so, you..." – "Without a care,
I just kept singing, all the summer long."
"You kept singing? Well, that's the point:
Now go and dance for a while."

XIII
The Liar

From distant wanderings returning,
A certain nobleman (and maybe even a prince),
Walking in a field with his friend,
Boasted extravagantly about where he had been,
And to true stories added countless embellishments.
"No," he said, "the sort of things that I have seen

I really shall not see again.
What sort of country do we have here?
Now it is cold, then it is very hot;
Now there is no sun, then it shines too brightly.
But over there is a real paradise!
Just to think about it brings such joy to the soul!
Neither fur coats nor candles are ever needed:
You never know the darkness of night,
And all through God's year you see only the May day.
No one there either plants or sows;
And you only have to look to see things grow and ripen!
So, for example, in Rome I saw a cucumber:
Oh, my Creator!
I cannot remember ever seeing anything like it.
Can you believe it? Well, really, it was the size
of a mountain."
"What a marvel!" his friend replied.
"Miracles are found everywhere in the world;
But not by everyone are they always noticed.
We ourselves are now approaching a miracle,
The like of which I dare say you have never seen.
I shall tell you about it.
There, do you see that bridge across the river,
Whither lies our way? Though in appearance it is simple,
It has a miraculous property:
There is not a single liar who dares to cross it:
Before he reaches half-way,
It collapses and he falls into the water;
But he who does not lie
Crosses it even, perhaps, while riding in a carriage."
"What kind of river is it?"
"Well, not shallow.

So you see, my friend, there is nothing like it in the world.
Though your Roman cucumber is huge, no dispute about that,
Indeed, the size of a mountain, it seems – did you not say
that about it?"
"Perhaps not a mountain, but certainly the size of a house."
"Difficult to believe!
But, however miraculous,
After all, miraculous too is the bridge, across which
we shall walk,
In that it in no way supports a liar;
And just this spring
There fell off it (all the town knows this)
Two journalists and a tailor.
Undoubtedly, a cucumber even the size of a house
Is a wonder, if it is true."
"Well, perhaps it is not such a wonder;
You see, one has to know how things are:
Do not think that everywhere there are mansions like ours;
The kind of houses to be found there
Are such as only two people can get into;
And then they can neither stand nor sit."
"Let it be so, but still one must confess,
That it is no sin to consider your cucumber a miracle,
In which two people may be accommodated.
However, our bridge is of such a nature
That a liar will not take five steps on it
Before falling straightaway into the water.
Though your Roman cucumber is indeed wonderful…"
"Well, listen," the Liar now interrupted,
Rather than use the bridge, why don't we look
for a better crossing?"

XIV
The Eagle and the Bee

Happy is he who labours in a great endeavour.
He even gains strength from knowing
That the whole world is a witness to his exploits.
But that one is just as estimable who engages in humble work.
For all his labours, for all his anxieties,
He is tempted by neither glory nor honour,
And is animated by a single thought:
To labour for the common good.

Seeing how a Bee was bustling around a little flower,
An Eagle once said to her disdainfully:
"How pitiful you are to me, poor thing,
With all your work, and with your skill!
Thousands of you in the hive all summer fashion a honeycomb;
And who on earth afterwards will want to identify
And single out your contribution?
I really shall never understand the desire
To labour a whole lifetime. And to what end?
To die obscurely with all the others.
What a difference between us!
When, spreading my vast wings,
I float beneath the clouds,
Then everywhere I sow fear:
Birds dare not rise from the ground,
Shepherds keep watch on their well-fed flocks;
And even nimble fallow-deer do not dare on the fields,
Catching sight of me, to show themselves."

The Bee replied: "All praise and honour to you!
And may Zeus prolong his munificence to you.
But I, having been born to labour for the common weal,
    Do not seek to single out my share;
I take comfort from knowing that, in our honeycomb,
    Even a drop of the honey is mine."

XV
The Hare on the Hunt

    A big crowd of animals
    Got together and caught a bear;
    They felled him on the open field –
    And were deciding among themselves
    Who was to receive what in reward.
A Hare came forward and tugged at the bear's ear.
    "Well, well, you, slant-eyed creature,"
They shouted at him. "Where did you come from?
    No one saw you on the hunt."
    "Look, brothers," the Hare replied.
"Who do you think frightened the beast out of the woods,
And drove it straight to you on the field, if not I?"
Although such boasting was too transparent,
    Still, it seemed so amusing,
That a tuft of the bear's ear was given to the Hare.

Though they laugh at a braggart,
He often receives his share of the spoils.

XVI
The Pike and the Cat

If a shoe-maker undertakes to bake pies,
And a pastry-cook to stitch boots,
Then the proceedings will not go well;
And indeed it has been noticed a hundred times
That he who loves to take up someone else's trade
Is always more stubborn and quarrelsome than others:
He would rather destroy the whole enterprise,
And is sooner happy
To become a laughing-stock of the world,
Than to ask for or listen to the intelligent advice
Of honest and knowledgeable people.

———

The thought occurred to a sharp-toothed Pike
To take up the feline trade.
I do not know whether it was the devil
That tormented her with envy,
Or whether she was bored with a fishy diet;
But she just bethought herself of asking a Cat
To take her with him on a hunt –
To catch mice in the barn.
"But wait, do you know this work, dear?"
The Cat, Vaska, said to the Pike.
"Watch out, my friend, that you don't disgrace yourself:
For good reason is it said
That a craftsman knows his trade."
"Enough, dear neighbour! Mice: that's nothing!
We even used to catch ruff."
"Well, let's go. Good luck!" They went to work.

The Cat enjoyed himself, ate his fill,
And went to see how his friend was getting on;
But the Pike, barely alive, lay with gaping mouth:
Rats had bitten off and eaten her tail.
Now, seeing that the Pike was not at all equal to the task,
The Cat pulled her back to the pond half-dead.
It served her right! Let this, Pike,
Be a lesson to you:
From now on be more intelligent,
And don't go after mice.

XVII
The Wolf and the Cuckoo

"Goodbye, neighbour!" a Wolf said to a Cuckoo.
"I was mistaken to think this place would be peaceful.
You have all the same people and dogs,
Each more wicked than the other;
Even an angel could not avoid fighting with them."
"But do you have far to go?
And where can those pious inhabitants be found,
With whom you are hoping to live so amicably?"
"Oh, I am going straight
To the happy Arcadian woods.
That's the place to be, my friend!
There, they say that war is unknown;
People are as meek as lambs,
And the rivers flow with milk;
Well, in short, the golden times reign!
All behave like brothers, one with another,
And they say the dogs there don't even bark,

Let alone bite.
So tell me yourself, dear,
Would it not be nice, even in your dreams,
To see yourself in such a peaceful land?
Goodbye! Remember me kindly.
Oh, what a life I shall live there!
In harmony, in contentment, in abundance.
Not, like here – always looking behind me by day,
And by night being unable to sleep peacefully."
"Pleasant journey, my dear neighbour!"
The Cuckoo replied. "And your own nature and your teeth,
Will you leave those here, or take them with you?"
"What! Leave them here? What nonsense!"
"Then, mark my words, you will not be long for this world."

The worse a nature people have,
The more they shout and complain about others:
Wherever they turn they see unkindness,
But are themselves the ones who get on with nobody.

XVIII
The Cock and the Pearl

Digging through a pile of manure,
A Cockerel found a Pearl,
And said: "What's this for?
What a useless thing!
Is it not stupid that it is prized so highly?
I myself, really, would be much happier
With a grain of barley-corn: though not so beautiful,
It is at least nourishing."

Ignoramuses make exactly the same judgments:
Not seeing the value of a thing, they consider it useless.

XIX
The Peasant and the Labourer

When misfortune strikes,
We are eager to appeal to others
To come to our aid;
But no sooner are we delivered from trouble
Than we often abuse those very ones who helped us.
We assess their actions one by one,
And if in our eyes they are not guilty,
Then it is a miracle!

An old Peasant man and a Labourer
Were walking through a grove towards dusk,
Home, to the village, from haymaking,
When suddenly they met a bear face to face.
The Peasant did not even have time to cry out
Before the bear fell upon him.
The bear crushed him, turned him over, struck him,
And was looking for a place to finish him off.
The old man's end seemed to have come.
"Stepanushka, my dear, don't desert me,"
He begged the Labourer from beneath the bear.
So, like a new Hercules, the Labourer,
Having summoned all the strength that was in him,

Struck the bear with an axe, taking away half its skull,
And pierced its belly with an iron pitch-fork.
The bear let out a roar, fell lifelessly and died.
Tragedy was averted. But when the Peasant rose,
He began to swear at the Labourer.
Poor Stepan was taken aback.
"For goodness sake," he said, "how do I deserve this abuse?"
"Blockhead! It is stupid for you to be pleased with yourself:
You struck the bear too violently, and damaged its skin!"

XX

The Convoy

A Convoy conveying pots was trundling along,
And had to descend a steep hill.
Here, having given up waiting for the others,
The driver of the first cart gently began to move.
His cautious horse almost had the cart on its back,
Not letting it roll out of control;
But the horse behind, a young one,
Scolded the other at every step:
"Hey, admirable steed, what a marvel you are!
Look: he clings to the path like a lobster;
He almost tripped on a stone. He's walking sideways, weaving!
Be bolder! There's another jolt for him!
He should have gone to the left there.
What an ass! It would be different if it were uphill,
Or at night;
But this is downhill, and during the day.
One can lose patience just watching.
You should carry water if you lack the skill for this work!

Just look at me, how I shall dash down!
Don't worry, I shall not waste a minute,
And I shall not pull my cart, but roll it down."
Here, arching his back and straining his chest,
The young horse set out along the path with the cart;
But no sooner had he started to descend the hill
Than the cart began to roll with increasing speed;
It pushed the horse from behind, throwing him from
side to side;
The horse set off at full tilt,
Running with abandon;
Over stones and ruts, jolting the cart,
He galloped along;
But he went too much to the side,
And ended up, with the cart, in the ditch.
So it was goodbye to the owner's pots.

―――――――

People also have much the same weakness:
Everything another does seems to them a mistake;
But when they themselves become involved
The outcome can often be twice as bad.

XXI
The Young Crow

An Eagle
From beneath the heavens swooped down on a flock
And snatched a lamb.
A young Crow who was nearby, watching,
Was greatly impressed, but thought:

"If one does something, surely one should do it properly;
Otherwise, why soil one's claws?
Evidently even eagles can be witless.
I mean, are there just lambs in the flock?
When I want a meal
I shall swoop down
And pick up a really choice specimen."
So the Crow rose over the flock
And on it cast a greedy glance:
He scrutinised a multitude of lambs and rams and sheep,
And finally selected a ram.
And what a ram! Very plump, very mature;
A ram which would have challenged even a healthy wolf.
Having positioned himself, the Crow dived,
And with all his strength dug his claws into the ram's wool.
But then he realised that the prey was not for him.
Worst of all, the ram had
Such a very shaggy coat –
Thick, dishevelled, matted –
That our winged nincompoop could not extract his claws.
And the exploit finished thus, that he fell into captivity.
The shepherds easily plucked him from the ram,
And so that he could not fly,
Cropped his wings,
And gave him as a plaything to the children.

It is quite often the same with people:
If a petty thief
Imitates a big thief,
The big thief escapes, and the petty thief is punished.

XXII
The Elephant as Governor

If one is noble and strong,
But not intelligent,
Then it is bad if one has a kind heart.

An Elephant was appointed Governor of the forest.
Elephants are thought to be an intelligent breed,
But no species is without an exception.
Our Governor was by nature fat,
But unusually for an Elephant he was simple-minded;
He would not on purpose have hurt a fly.
Now the kind Governor saw
A complaint sent in to the Department by the sheep,
Who reported that wolves were tearing off their skin.
"Oh, the rogues!" shouted the Elephant. "What a crime!
Who gave them permission for this?"
But the wolves replied: "Forgive us, our father!
Was it not you who gave us permission to collect
A light quitrent from the sheep for our winter coats?
But they complain, because sheep are stupid.
All we want is to take from each sheep one skin,
And they begrudge us even that."
"Well, so be it," said the Elephant. "But watch out!
I shall not tolerate wrongdoing in anyone.
Do as you say: take a skin from each sheep,
But don't take a hair more."

XXIII
The Ass and the Nightingale

An Ass met a Nightingale,
And said to him: "Listen, my friend!
They say you are a very accomplished singer:
I would very much like to judge for myself,
Having heard your song,
Whether your skill is really so great."
So the Nightingale began to display his art:
He began to trill, to whistle;
A thousand sustained harmonies flowed from his throat;
In time, softly, the song subsided,
And in the distance was heard like a delicate reed-pipe.
Then insistent staccato notes resounded
through the grove,
And everything was captivated
By the favourite singer of Aurora;
The breezes abated, bird choruses fell silent,
And flocks lay down, scarcely breathing.
The shepherd listened in admiration,
And only from time to time,
Listening to the Nightingale, smiled at the shepherdess.
The singer finished.
The Ass, standing stolidly, forehead lowered
to the ground, said,
"To say truly, that is tolerable;
It is possible to listen to you without becoming too bored;
But it is a pity that unacquainted
Are you with our cockerel:
You would become even better at singing

If you were to study his art for a while."
Having heard this judgment, my poor Nightingale
Flew up and – flew away to the end of the world.

———————

God save us from such judgments.

Book Three

I
The Tax-Collector and the Cobbler

A rich Tax-Collector lived in a great mansion;
He ate the best food and drank well;
Each day gave feasts, banquets;
Of his wealth there was no estimate.
In his house were whatever delicacies you could wish for,
All in abundance, beyond measure.
In a word, it seemed like paradise in his home.
In only one way did the Tax-Collector suffer:
He did not get enough sleep.
Whether he already feared the judgment of God,
Or was simply afraid to lose his money,
Somehow he just could not get a good night's sleep.
And moreover, though sometimes
Towards dawn he would doze, yet another misfortune beset him:
God gave him a singer for a neighbour.
Opposite him in the street lived a pauper in a shack,
A Cobbler, but such a songster and cheerful soul
That from dawn, even until supper,
And then from supper until night, he ceaselessly sang,
And in no way let the rich man sleep.
What could be done to deal with this neighbour,
So as to make him stop singing?
The Tax-Collector could not order him to stop;
He begged him, but such entreaties did not avail.

Finally an idea occurred to him, and he sent for his
neighbour.
The neighbour arrived.
"Dear friend, hello!" said the Tax-Collector.
"You wished to speak to me, sir?"
"Well, Klim, how are things going, my friend?"
(Those who have a need of someone always learn his name.)
"Things, master? Well, not bad!"
"So is it because you are happy that you sing?
Is it because you have a happy life?"
"It is a sin before God to grumble, but it is not surprising:
I have always had enough work;
My wife is a good woman, and young;
And with a good wife – who does not know this? –
One always somehow lives more happily."
"And is there money enough?"
"Well no, there is usually none to spare,
But then there are no unnecessary expenses."
"So then, my friend, you do not wish to be richer?"
"I do not say that, though I thank God even for what I have.
But you yourself, master, know that Man, while he lives,
Keeps wanting more: this is what life is like.
I would think that, to you, even your riches are too little;
Certainly it would do me no harm to be richer."
"You talk sense, my friend:
Though with riches also come cares,
And though they say that poverty is not a vice,
Still, if one is to suffer, it is better to do so with riches.
So take this: here is a sack of *roubles* for you:
I admire you for your honesty.
Go now: God has willed that you become rich with my help.
But take care that you do not squander this money:

Keep it in case of need.
Here are five hundred *roubles*, all counted and correct.
Goodbye!"
My Cobbler, grasping the sack, went home quickly:
Not running, but floating;
He hurried along with the gift under his apron,
And that very night in the cellar
Buried the sack – and with it his happiness.
Now, not only were there no songs – what happened to his sleep?
(Even he became acquainted with insomnia!)
He was suspicious of everything, and everything worried him:
No sooner did a cat begin to scratch at night
Than he believed that a thief had come;
He would go all cold, and bend an ear;
Well, in a word, the life went out of him:
The only thing to do was to throw himself in the river.
The Cobbler struggled and struggled;
And finally he came to his senses:
He ran with the sack to the Tax-Collector
And said: "Thank you for kindness:
Here is your sack, take it back:
Until now I had not known how badly some sleep.
Live with your riches,
But for me, for my songs and for my sleep,
Millions are not necessary."

II

A Peasant in Trouble

A thief one autumn night came into a Peasant's house.
He got into the storeroom

And freely ransacked the whole place,
Brazenly stole all that he could.
Truth to tell, what conscience has a thief?
Well, so our Peasant, poor devil,
Went to bed a rich man and rose such a pauper
That he might have had to go begging.
God forbid that anyone should wake up so badly!
The Peasant grieved for his loss and bewailed his fate;
He summoned his family and friends,
All his neighbours and relations.
"Is it possible," he said, "to help me in my misfortune?"
Here, all started to talk to the man,
And give their wise advice.
Cousin Karpich said: "Ah, my dear fellow,
There was no need for you to boast to the world
That you were so rich."
Brother-in-law Klimich said, "In the future, my dear boy,
Try to build the storeroom much closer to the house."
"Oh, friends, this is not at all so," said his neighbour Foka.
"The trouble is not that the storeroom is far away;
Rather, you should keep vicious guard-dogs in the yard;
Do take any of my bitch Zhuchka's pups:
With all my heart I would give them to my dear neighbour,
Rather than drown them."
In short, all the relatives and kind friends
Offered as much useful advice as they could.
But not one gave the poor man any practical help.

Thus it is in life: if you fall into need,
Try to appeal to friends:
They will advise you in all sorts of ways,

But as soon as you hint at help for your predicament,
Then the best friend will be deaf to it.

III
The Home-Owner and the Mice

If in your house someone begins to steal,
But you cannot identify the thief,
Then guard against slandering
Or punishing everyone indiscriminately.
You will not stop the thief,
And will not reform him;
You will only cause good servants to run from the house,
And will fall from a lesser into a greater misfortune.

A Merchant built storerooms
And in them placed all his provisions;
But so that a colony of mice could not become established
He introduced a force of cats.
The Merchant was untroubled by mice:
The cats patrolled the storerooms day and night.
And all would have been well,
Except that a thief made his appearance in the patrols.
Among cats, as among people (who does not know this?)
Are individuals who are not without sin.
But rather than lie in wait for the thief,
And punish him, and spare the innocent,
My Home-Owner gave the order for all the cats to be thrashed.
Having heard this unwarranted sentence,
Both the innocent and the guilty

Quickly ran from the house.
My Merchant was left without cats.
But this was just what the mice wanted, and expected:
As soon as the cats left they moved into the storeroom,
And in two or three weeks ate all the provisions.

IV

The Elephant and the Pug

Along the street an Elephant was being led,
Probably as an exhibit.
It is well known that people are fascinated by elephants,
So behind the beast followed a crowd of idlers.
As if from nowhere a Pug appeared
And, seeing the Elephant, rushed towards it,
Barking, and yelping, and lungeing,
And clearly spoiling for a fight.
"Neighbour, stop disgracing yourself,"
Said a mongrel to the Pug. "Is it for you to take on an Elephant?
Look, you are already wheezing, but he just walks on ahead,
And does not even notice your barking."
"So what!" the Pug replied.
"This is just to give me courage,
So that, quite without fighting,
I can be considered a big bully.
Now let the other dogs say:
'Hey, that Pug – she must be strong,
To bark at an Elephant!'"

V

The Wolf and the Wolf-cub

A Wolf, having started little by little to train a Cub
To live by the ancestral trade,
Sent him to take a walk along the edge of the forest,
And told him while there to be diligent in observing
Where, at the expense of the shepherd,
And even if it meant sinning,
They might not have some luck to dine or sup.
The pupil arrived home and said:
"Let's go there quickly together!
Supper is ready; nothing can be more certain:
There, beneath the mountain,
There are grazing sheep, each one fatter than the last;
One has only to carry off and eat any of them;
There are so many, they cannot be counted."
"Wait a moment," the Wolf said. "First I have to know,
What sort of shepherd is guarding the flock."
"Well, they say he is not bad: caring and clever;
However, I went all around the flock
And studied the dogs: it seems
They are all thin, and unhealthy and quiet."
"This report," the old Wolf said,
"Does not make the flock seem appealing;
If the shepherd really were good,
He would not keep bad dogs,
And straightaway we would get into trouble.
Let's go elsewhere: I shall bring you to a flock
Where there will be less chance of us losing our skins.
Though there are many dogs around that flock,

The shepherd himself is a fool,
And where the shepherd is a fool, there even
the dogs are fools."

VI
The Monkey

Labour as you wish,
But don't hope to gain
Either gratitude or fame,
If in your labour there is neither profit nor amusement.

A peasant at dawn with a plough
Was labouring over his patch,
Was labouring so intensively
That the sweat was rolling thick and fast.
Yes, the peasant was a real worker.
As a result, from all who passed
There came thanks and praise.
This made a Monkey envious.
Praise is wonderful – how could one not wish for it? –
So the monkey decided also to labour:
She found a wooden block and started to busy herself over it.
She worked at it tirelessly:
Now she carried the block,
Holding it this way and that,
Then she dragged it, then rolled it;
The sweat poured from the poor thing like a river.
She was panting, gasping for breath;
But still she heard no praise from anyone.

It was no wonder, my dear!
You laboured much, but there was no benefit in it.

VII
The Bag

On the floor of an entrance hall, in the corner,
An empty Bag lay quite forgotten.
The very lowest servants
Had often used it to wipe their feet.
But suddenly our Bag was honoured:
It was stuffed with gold coins,
And placed now in safety in a fettered casket.
The master of the house himself treasured it,
And guarded it in such a way that on it
He allowed neither a wind to blow, nor a fly to alight;
Moreover, all the town came to hear of the Bag:
If a friend arrived at the master's house,
Respectful talk about the Bag straightaway began;
And if it were open, then everybody looked admiringly at it.
Whenever anyone sat down next to it,
He began to pat or stroke it.
Seeing that it had increased so much in honour,
The Bag began to glory in its reputation,
Began to try to be clever, to give itself airs.
The Bag began to speak, and began to talk nonsense.
It gave orders and made judgments about everything:
This was really not so… and that one was a fool,
And from the other will come no good…
All just listened to it, open-mouthed,
Though it talked such nonsense as was painful to hear.

But people have, unfortunately, this flaw:
That they will marvel at a Bag with gold coins,
No matter what it says.
But was the Bag long considered clever and respected?
And was it long pampered?
Only while gold coins were taken from it;
Then it was discarded, and not a word more said about it.

We wish to offend no one with this fable;
But how many such Bags are there
Among tax-collectors
Who once served as lowly messengers;
Or among card players,
For whom a *rouble* used to be a rarity,
And who have only just managed to become rich,
But are now friends with counts and princes,
And casually play boston with grandees,
In whose entrance hall they once did not dare to sit?
Big deal – a million!
But don't be so proud, my friends.
Shall I quietly tell you the truth?
God forbid, but if you are ruined,
You will be treated exactly the same as the Bag.

VIII
The Cat and the Cook

A certain Cook, a literate man,
Left his kitchen for the tavern
(He was devout, and on this day was a relative's wake).

At home, to guard the edibles from mice,
He left a Cat.
But on returning, what did he see? On the floor
Were the remains of a pie; in the corner, Vaska the Cat
Was lying behind a vinegar cask,
Purring and growling, labouring over a chicken.
"Oh, you glutton! Oh, scoundrel!"
The Cook upbraided Vaska.
"Are you not ashamed before the very walls,
Let alone before people?"
(But Vaska just went on eating the chicken.)
"Look, you've been a well-behaved cat till now –
I used to show you off as an example of obedience –
But you... oh, what a disgrace!
Now all the neighbours will say:
'Cat-Vaska is a rogue! Cat-Vaska is a thief!
One must not let that Vaska into the yard,
Let alone the kitchen.
He is like a greedy wolf in the sheep-fold.
He is rotten, he is a plague, he is scum in this place!'"
(Vaska listened. And went on eating.)
And so my rhetorician, giving free rein to the flow of words,
Found no end to his moral lecture.
But what happened? While he was holding forth,
Cat-Vaska finished the roast.

I would advise another cook
To chisel on the wall:
Do not waste words in vain,
When what is needed is action.

IX
The Lion and the Mosquito

Do not laugh at the weak,
And do not offend the defenceless.
Weak enemies sometimes take strong revenge:
So do not think of relying too much on your strength.
Listen here to a fable about this,
About how badly a Lion was punished by a Mosquito
for arrogance.
This is what I happened to hear about that:
A Lion displayed cold contempt for a Mosquito;
Not prepared to suffer insults, the Mosquito
was filled with malice,
And declared war on the Lion.
The Warrior was his own trumpeter,
and with a penetrating whine,
Challenged the Lion to mortal combat.
The Lion laughed, but our Mosquito was not jesting:
He blared his intentions from the Lion's back,
from his eyes, his ears,
And having seen a place, and finding a time,
Descended on the Lion like an eagle,
And with all his might stung the beast on the lower back.
The Lion shook himself and lashed his tail at the Trumpeter.
Our Mosquito was evasive, and certainly not afraid:
He sat on the Lion's very forehead, and sucked the Lion's blood.
The Lion twisted his head, the Lion shook his mane;
But our hero paid no attention:
Now he flew into the Lion's nose, then he stung him in the ear.
The Lion was senseless with anger, and raised a frightful howl,

Gnashing his teeth in fury and tearing the ground with his claws.
A terrible roar shook the surrounding forest,
Instilling fear into all the animals, who ran away to hide.
They fled with the panic they might feel
When fleeing a flood or fire.
And who was the cause of their troubles?
The Mosquito was responsible for it all!
The Lion thrashed around, lurched from side to side,
And having worn himself out,
Crashed to the ground and sued for peace.
The Mosquito had sated his fury: he granted surcease
to the Lion:
Suddenly, from Achilles he was transformed into Peacemaker,
And flew away to proclaim his victory through the forest.

X

The Market Gardener and the Philosopher

In spring, in his vegetable beds, a Market Gardener dug
As if he were digging up treasure:
That peasant was a zealous worker,
Strapping and young, to judge by appearance;
Under the cucumbers alone he dug up some fifty beds.
Next door to him lived an enthusiast
For vegetable and flower gardens,
A great gas-bag who was called the friend of nature:
A half-educated Philosopher
Whose knowledge of kitchen gardens came only from books.
However, he bethought himself of setting up his own patch,
And also planting cucumbers;
But meanwhile, he joked thus to his neighbour:

"My friend, you may sweat if you like,
But I shall outdo you in the work,
And compared to mine your kitchen garden
Will seem a wasteland.
Yes, truth to say, I am even surprised
That your miserable little patch produces anything at all.
How have you not yet gone broke?
I suppose you have studied no science, then?"
"I really have had no time," was the neighbour's reply.
"Diligence, skill, labour – those are all my sciences;
With them alone God gives me food."
"Ignoramus! Do you dare to revolt against science?"
"No, your honour, don't twist my words.
If you undertake something sensible,
I am always ready to learn from you."
"Well, let's just wait for summer."
"But your honour, is it not time you got down to work?
I have already sowed and planted something;
Yet you have not dug up even a single bed."
"No, I have not yet started digging; I have had no time:
I read a lot, and have read
About the best instruments to use,
Whether to turn up the beds with a spade, or a plough, or a hoe.
But there is still plenty of time."
"Perhaps for you," the other replied, "but for me time does not wait."
And he straightaway parted from his neighbour.
Having taken his spade, the Philosopher went home.
He read, made copious notes, investigated,
And rooted about both in his books and his beds.
From morning till night he laboured.
Hardly had he finished one task,

When something else came up in the beds:
In magazines he kept finding new ideas;
He kept digging up, transplanting, doing things in a new way.
How did it end?
All of the Gardener's vegetables grew and ripened:
He finished the year successfully and made a profit;
But the Philosopher was left without cucumbers.

XI
The Peasant and the Fox

"Tell me, my friend, what is this passion you have
For stealing hens?"
A Peasant asked a Fox, having met her.
"I sincerely pity you!
Listen, there are just the two of us now;
I shall be frank with you: surely in your behaviour
There is not a bit of good.
Not only is stealing shameful and a sin,
For which everyone berates you,
But there is not a single day
When, for dinner or supper, you do not fear
To lose your life in the hen house!
Well, are all the hens worth it?"
"Who indeed," replied the Fox, "would find such a life tolerable?
It all distresses me so much
That I do not even find the food tasty.
I would have you know that in my heart of hearts I am honest!
But what can I do? I have needs, children to support;
Besides, dear neighbour, it sometimes occurs to me to wonder –
Although my trade hurts me like a sharp knife –

Whether I am the only one in the world who lives by stealing."
"Well, then," the Peasant said, "if indeed you do not lie,
I shall save you from sin,
And shall provide you with honest food;
Enter my service, protecting my hen-house from foxes:
Who but a fox knows all the tricks of foxes?
And then you will not suffer need in anything,
And will stay with me to live off the fat of the land."
The bargain was agreed;
And from that very hour the Fox mounted guard.
The Fox had an easy life at the Peasant's;
The Peasant was rich, the Fox had enough of everything;
The Fox was better fed than ever, and put on weight,
And yet she did not become more honest:
She soon grew tired of unstolen food,
And ended her employment like this:
Having chosen the darkest night,
She killed all the hens in the hen-house.

That one who has a conscience and a code,
Will neither cheat nor steal,
Whatever his need;
But give even a million to a thief –
And he will not stop thieving.

XII
The Upbringing of a Lion

To a Lion, the monarch of the forest, God granted a son.
You know what animals are like:

They are not like us – if we have a year-old child,
Even if he is royal, he is stupid, weak and small;
But a year-old Lion cub
Long ago came out of the cradle.
So after a year the Lion-father began to have
serious thoughts:
So as not to have a boor for a son,
Not to have him lacking in kingly nature,
So that when he came to rule the realm
The animals would not blame the father because of the son,
Whom could he engage, or compel,
To take on the training of the Prince as a Tsar?
He could apprentice him to a fox – the fox is clever,
But she is a great enthusiast for lying;
And a liar in any walk of life brings trouble;
So this, thought the Tsar, would not be a Tsar-like upbringing.
He could send him to the Mole – but the rumour was
That the Mole loves order in everything:
He does not take a step without feeling his way,
And any seed for his table
He himself cleans, and himself peels;
And, in short, the rumour went,
That the Mole is a great animal in small matters;
Besides, the Mole-like eyes under the nose are near-sighted,
And see nothing in the distance;
No: the Mole's qualities may be good, but only for himself:
The leonine kingdom was much bigger than a burrow.
Why not take on a Snow leopard?
The Snow leopard is courageous and strong;
And moreover he is a great tactician;
But the Snow leopard knows nothing of policy:
He does not at all understand civil law.

What kind of example would he set as a ruler?
A Tsar has to be a judge, a minister and a warrior;
But the Snow leopard is good only for furious play,
So he is simply unworthy to teach royal children.
In short: all animals, and even the Elephant himself
(Who was respected in the forest, as in Greece was Plato),
To the Lion seemed inadequate and uneducated.
Luckily or not (we shall see this shortly),
Having heard about the Tsar's trouble,
Another such Tsar – a feathered Tsar – an Eagle,
Who desired the friendship and goodwill of the Tsar,
Undertook to do him a favour,
And himself volunteered to educate the Lion-cub.
It was as if a heavy load had been lifted from the Tsar's shoulders.
Indeed: what, it seemed, could have been better
Than to find a Tsar in a teacher for the Tsarevitch?
So he prepared the Lion-cub,
And sent him to the Eagle to learn how to reign.
A year passed, then two; meanwhile,
Whoever asked about the Lion-cub heard only praise:
All the birds reported miracles about him in the woods.
The appointed year finally arrived;
The Lion-king sent for his son.
The son came, and the Tsar summoned all the animals,
Called together both the big and the small.
He kissed his son, embraced him,
And spoke to him thus: "Beloved son, you are my sole heir.
I am now looking into the grave, while you are only
entering upon life:
So I shall gladly give you the kingdom.
Only, tell us now in the presence of all,
What you have learned, what you know,

And how you expect to make your subjects happy."
"Papa," replied the son, "I know what no one here knows:
I know, from the eagle to the quail,
What birds are more numerous, and where they are to be found;
Which of them lives on what, and the eggs that they lay.
All the needs of birds I know, to the smallest detail.
Here from my teacher is a certificate for you:
When it comes to birds,
With good reason do they say that I am very knowledgeable.
When you intend to entrust the government to me,
Then straightaway I shall begin to teach the animals how to build nests."
Here, the Tsar and all the animals groaned;
The Council despaired:
Too late did the old Lion suddenly realise,
That the Lion-cub had just learned trifles,
And that he was talking nonsense.
There was no great advantage in knowing about the life of birds,
If nature intended one to reign over animals.
The most important lesson for a Tsar
Is to know the nature of his people,
And the potential of his land.

XIII
The Old Man and Three Youths

An Old Man was getting ready to plant a sapling.
"You could certainly build a hut, but why plant a tree at your age,
When your life is already ebbing away!"
Thus, laughing in the face of the Old Man,

Reasoned three grown-up neighbouring Youths.
"In order for you to see the fruit of your labour
   You would have to live two centuries.
Do you really think you are a second Methuselah?
   Abandon, Old Man, your work:
Is it for you to undertake such long-term projects?
   There is now hardly enough time left to you.
Such doings would be understandable in us:
We are young, we radiate strength and power,
But the time comes for an Old Man to think about the grave."
   "Friends!" the Old Man humbly replied.
"Since childhood I have been accustomed to hard work;
   And if, from what I am about to do,
   I do not myself expect to benefit,
Then I declare I would just as willingly see it through.
He who is wise labours not just for himself.
   I rejoice in the planting of a tree;
   And if I myself do not live to see it grown
Then my grandson one day may enjoy its shade,
   And this for me would be fruit indeed.
   Is it possible to predict in advance
   Who of us here will survive whom?
Does death take account of youth, strength,
      Or the charms of a face?
Ah, in my long life I have seen off to the grave
The most beautiful girls and the strongest youths!
Who knows: it may be that your hour is even closer,
And that the damp earth will cover you first."
As the Old Man said, so afterwards it proved.
   One of the Youths took ship in trade;
   Fortune at first favoured him with hope,
   But in a storm his ship broke up;

Hope and the sailor both perished at sea.
Another, in foreign lands,
Having succumbed to the allure of vice,
Paid for luxury, comfort and passion,
First with his health, then with his life.
And the third – on a hot day he quaffed a cold drink,
And took to his bed: he was entrusted to skilled doctors –
Who doctored him to death.
Having learned about their end,
Our kind Old Man mourned for all three.

XIV
The Tree

Seeing a peasant who was carrying an axe,
A young Tree said, "My friend!
Be so good as to cut down the wood around me.
I cannot grow as I should:
Neither is the light of the sun visible to me,
Nor is there space for my roots,
Nor is there freedom for the breezes around me,
Such a canopy the wood deigned to weave!
Were it not such a hindrance to my growth,
In a year I would become an ornament to this land,
And with my shade would cover all the valley;
But now I am thin, almost like a stick."
The peasant took up his axe,
And to the Tree, as to a friend,
He rendered a service.
Around the sapling a big expanse was cleared;
But not for long was the Tree to rejoice.

Now the sun scorched him,
Then he was lashed by hail and rain,
And at last he was felled by the wind.
"Foolish one!" a snake now said to him.
"Are you not the author of your own misfortune?
If you had grown, sheltered by the wood,
Neither baking heat nor winds would have damaged you.
The old trees would have protected you.
Then one day there would not be such trees:
Their time would have come,
And you in your turn would have begun to grow;
You would have grown strong, and become so well-rooted
That the present misfortune would not have happened:
You would have been able to withstand the storm."

XV
The Geese

With a very long stick,
A peasant was driving Geese to town to sell;
And, to be quite truthful,
Was not very politely abusing the flock:
He was hurrying for profit on market day
(And, where profit is concerned,
It is not only geese, but people who suffer).
I do not blame the peasant;
But the Geese felt differently about this
And, meeting with a traveller on the way,
Here is how they complained about the peasant:
"Where can you find birds more unfortunate than us?
The peasant so orders us about,

And drives us as if we were ordinary geese;
But this ignoramus does not understand
That he owes us respect,
Because our noble race is descended from those Geese
To whom long ago Rome was indebted for salvation.
There, even festivals are held in our honour!"
"And what are you yourselves distinguished for?"
the traveller asked.
"Well, our ancestors…"
"I know, I've read all about it; but I wish to know,
Of what use are you yourselves?.."
"But our ancestors saved Rome!"
"That is indeed so; but what of suchlike importance
have *you* done?"
"We? Nothing!"
"So what good are you? Leave your ancestors in peace:
It is right to honour them;
But you, my friends, are suitable only as fried meat."

I could explain this fable,
But I do not wish to tease the Geese.

XVI
The Pig

A Pig once intruded into a manor-house yard,
Loitered around the stables and kitchen,
Rolled about in the rubbish and the manure,
Wallowed up to the ears in the mud;
And, after visiting,

Went home as dirty as a pig.
"So then, Havronya, what did you see there?"
A shepherd asked the Pig.
"You know, the rumour goes,
That rich people have nothing but jewellery and pearls.
So is one thing really worth more than another in the house?"
Havronya grunted: "Well, really, that is nonsense.
I noticed no riches:
It was all just manure and rubbish;
And so, not sparing my snout,
I dug up there
All the back yard."

God forbid that I offend anyone by this comparison.
But how can I not call a literary critic Havronya,
Who, whatever he begins to analyse,
Has the gift to see only the bad?

XVII
The Fly and the Travellers

In July, in intense heat, at midday,
Over thick sand, uphill,
With luggage, and with the family of a nobleman,
A four-horse coach
Was lumbering along.
The horses were exhausted, and however the coachman drove them
They had to stop. He climbed down from the coach-box.
Then, this tormentor of the horses, and a footman,

Began to whip the animals from both sides.
But it did not help. There then crept from the carriage
The nobleman, his wife, their maid, their son and a tutor.
But the coach must have been heavily laden,
Because the horses, though they could move it on the flat,
Could in no way pull it uphill through the sand.
Now a Fly happened to be there. How could she not assist?
She set to work: she started buzzing with all her might.
Around the carriage she bustled;
Now she fussed around one horse's nose,
Now she bit the forehead of another;
Now, in place of the coachman, she sat on the box
Or, leaving the horses,
Darted here and there among the people;
Well, like a tax-collector at a trade fair she busied herself,
And only regretted that no one
In any way tried to help her.
The servants gossiped nonsensically, plodding along on foot;
The tutor and mistress whispered quietly together;
The master himself, having forgotten that he needed
to supervise,
Went with the maid to the forest to look for
mushrooms for dinner;
As for the Fly, she buzzed to everyone
That she alone was taking care of everything.
Meanwhile the poor horses, step by step, little by little,
Dragged the coach up to the flat road.
"Well," said the Fly, "now thank God!
Take your places, and a safe journey to you all;
I really need a rest:
My wings can hardly bear me."

There are a great many people in life
Who want to interfere everywhere,
And who love to bustle about where they are not asked.

XVIII
The Eagle and the Spider

Above the clouds an Eagle
To the summit of the Caucasian peaks soared.
There he sat on a hundred-year old cedar,
And admired the vast expanse under him.
It seemed that from there he could see the edge of the world:
Radiant, winding rivers flowed along the steppe,
And here and there groves and meadows flourished
In all their spring attire;
In the distance the angry Caspian Sea
Glimmered black as the wing of a crow.
The Eagle said to Jupiter:
"Praise to you, Zeus, that, creating the world,
You provided me with such an ability to fly
That I know nothing of inaccessible heights.
And that I look on the beauties of the world from that place
Whither no one else is able to fly."
"It seems you are quite a braggart,"
A spider replied to him from a twig.
"Do I, my friend, sit here lower than you?"
The Eagle looked: and indeed, a Spider,
Having spread a web above him,
Was busying himself on a twig.
It seemed to the Eagle that he was trying to hide the sun.

"How did you come to this height?" asked the Eagle.
"Even of those who are most courageous in flight,
Not all dare to set out hither;
But you, weak and without wings – did you really
crawl so high?"
"No, I would never have aspired to that."
"Well, so how did you come to be here?"
"Why, I clung to your tail,
And you yourself carried me from below.
But now I am able to hold on here by myself,
And so I would ask you not to glorify yourself in my presence,
And know, that I…"
Now a whirlwind, as if from nowhere,
Suddenly blew the Spider down again to the very ground.

I don't know how it seems to you,
But to me this Spider seems to resemble
One who, without intelligence and even without effort,
Drags himself up in the world holding on to the tail
of a great one.
He puffs out his chest,
As if God had provided him with an eagle's strength;
But a wind has only to blow,
And he is carried away like a cobweb.

XIX
The Doe and the Dervish

A young Doe, having lost her precious fawn,
Yet still having an udder heavy with milk,

Found in the woods two small wolf-cubs
And began to fulfil the sacred duty of a mother,
Feeding them with her milk.
A Dervish, living in the same forest as her,
Was astounded at her behaviour.
"Oh, foolish one!" he said. "Do you know
On whom you lavish your love and your milk?
Do you expect gratitude from such as them?
Perhaps one day (or do you not know their evil nature?)
They will shed your very blood."
"That may be so," replied the Doe,
"But I have not been thinking about that,
And do not wish to think of it:
To me now the maternal feeling alone is what counts:
My milk would be a burden to me,
Had I no young to suckle.

Such a genuinely good deed,
Without any recompense, is laudable.
To those who are kind, excess is a burden
If they do not share it with those near.

XX
The Dog

A landowner had a Dog that was naughty,
Though she was in want of nothing at all.
Any other animal would, with such a life,
Be entirely happy and content,
And would not think to steal.

But this Dog had a single passion:
Whatever meat she could grab,
In an instant she stole.
The master was unable to control her,
However hard he tried,
Until his friend stepped in
And offered sensible advice.
"Listen," he said, "though you seem to be strict,
You are only training the Dog to steal,
Because you always let her keep
What she takes.
In the future, why don't you beat her less,
And take away from her the stolen meat?"
No sooner had the master
Adopted this reasonable strategy
Than the Dog stopped stealing.

XXI
The Eagle and the Mole

Don't scorn anyone's advice,
But consider it first.

Having come from a distant land
To a dense forest, an Eagle and its mate
Decided to remain there for life;
And, having chosen a tall, spreading oak,
Began to build a nest for themselves in its crown,
Hoping to raise their young there in the summer.
A Mole, having heard about this,

Made bold to report to the Eagle
That the oak would not make a suitable abode,
As its roots had almost all rotted,
And that soon, perhaps, it would fall down;
So the Eagle should not seek to build a nest in it.
But does an Eagle take advice from a burrow?
And from a Mole! Where was the praise
For the Eagle's sharpsightedness?
And how does a Mole dare to meddle in the affairs
Of the king of birds!
So, not speaking any more with the Mole,
And scorning the advice, the Eagle quickly set to work.
And the king's new dwelling
Was soon ready for the queen.
All went happily: the Eagle indeed had young ones.
But what happened? One day, suddenly at dawn,
After hunting beneath the clouds, the Eagle hastened
With a rich breakfast to his family.
He saw that the oak had fallen,
Crushing his mate and young ones.
The Eagle was blind with grief.
"Unhappy one," he said.
"Because of pride, fate punished me so cruelly,
For not having heeded wise advice.
But could it have been expected
That an insignificant Mole would give good advice?"
"If you had not ignored me,"
The Mole said from his burrow, "you might
have remembered
That I dig my tunnels under the earth,
And that, finding myself near roots,
I can know more truly whether the tree is healthy."

Book Four

I
The Quartet

A naughty Monkey,
Donkey,
Goat,
And pigeon-toed Mishka, the Bear
Decided to form a quartet.
They got the music, a double-bass, viola and two violins,
And sat down in a meadow under lime trees
To charm the world with their art.
They applied the bows and scraped, to no avail.
"Stop, brothers, stop!" cried the Monkey. "Wait a minute!
How can we make music? You see, we are not sitting properly.
You with the bass, Misha dear, sit facing the viola;
I, the first violin, will sit facing the second;
Then the music will sound wonderful:
The woods and hills around will begin to dance!"
They took their places, and started to play;
But still the result was just cacophony.
"Be patient! I have found the secret,"
Cried the Donkey. "We shall probably get on better
If we sit in a row."
They agreed, and settled down in an orderly row;
But still no harmonious sound came out.
Now, more than before, they began to discuss,
And argue,

Who should sit where.
Hearing the noise, a nightingale flew to them,
And they all asked her to settle the matter.
"Perhaps," they said, "spare us a moment
To put our quartet in order:
We have the music, and we have the instruments,
Just tell us how we should sit."
"To be a musician one must have skill,"
The nightingale answered them,
"And ears a little more delicate than yours.
So you, friends, however you sit,
Will never serve as musicians."

II

The Leaves and The Roots

On a beautiful summer day,
Casting a shadow through the valley,
The Leaves on a tree whispered with the Zephyrs,
Boasting of their thick foliage.
And here is how they spoke about themselves to the Zephyrs:
"Is it not true that we are the greatest beauties
in all the valley?
That it is because of us that the tree is so rich and luxuriant,
So spreading and majestic?
What would dress it, without us? Well, truly,
We can praise ourselves without sin!
Do we not from the intense heat cover
The shepherd and the wanderer in cool shade?
And do we not with our loveliness
Attract here shepherdesses to dance?

In our foliage at dawn and sunset
The nightingale sings.
And you, Zephyrs, yourselves,
Hardly ever part from us."
"You might also give thanks to us down here,"
A voice said to them meekly from beneath the ground.
"Who dares to speak so impudently and arrogantly!"
Said the Leaves, rustling angrily on the tree.
"Who are you down there,
That you so insolently concern yourself with us."
"We are those who,
Spreading here in the dark,
Nourish you. Do you really not know this?
We are the roots of the tree, which allow you to flourish.
By all means flaunt yourself:
Good luck to you!
But just remember this difference between us:
That, with a new spring, new leaves will come into being;
But if the roots dry up,
There will be neither a tree, nor you."

III
The Wolf and the Fox

Willingly we give
What to ourselves is unnecessary.
I shall illustrate this with a fable,
Because the truth is clearer if only half-revealed.

———————

A Fox, having eaten chickens to her fill,
And stored away a nice little pile in reserve,

Lay down under a haystack for an evening nap.
She saw a hungry Wolf come plodding along to visit.
"What bad luck, neighbour!" he said.
"I have been unable anywhere to find even a bone;
I am so worn out with hunger.
The dogs are vicious, and the shepherd doesn't sleep.
The only thing to do is to hang myself!"
"Really?" – "Yes, it's true." – "My poor friend!
Would you like to eat some hay? Here is a whole stack;
I am willing to do my friend a service."
However, it was not hay her friend wanted – but meat.
Yet about the store the Fox said not a word.
And my grey marauder,
Having been shown such great kindness by his friend,
Went home hungry.

IV
The Kite

Launched under the clouds,
A Kite, noticing from on high
A moth in the valley, cried:
"Would you believe it! You are barely visible to me;
Confess – you are envious
That I fly so high."
"Envious? Indeed, no!
Mistakenly do you think so well of yourself.
Though high, you fly on a lead;
Such a life, my dear,
From happiness is far indeed;
I, on the other hand, while I fly less high,

Fly whither I want;
And so, unlike you, do not spend a lifetime
Frivolously snapping in the wind
As a pastime for another."

V
The Swan, the Pike and the Crayfish

When there is no agreement among friends,
Then their affairs will not run smoothly,
And all their efforts will prove to be in vain.

———————

A Swan, a Crayfish and a Pike once
Undertook to pull a luggage-laden cart;
The three of them all harnessed themselves to it;
They did their utmost, but the cart wouldn't move.
They should have found the load light;
But the Swan struggled into the air,
The Crayfish moved backwards,
And the Pike pulled towards the water.
Which of them was at fault,
And which blameless, is not for us to judge;
But the cart is still there today.

VI
The Starling

All have their own gifts,
But often, being tempted by someone else's success,

One starts doing a thing
To which one is not at all suited.
So my advice is this:
Take up that to which you are naturally suited,
If you wish to be a success.

A certain Starling in youth
Learned to sing so like a young goldfinch
That it was as if he himself had been born a goldfinch.
He amused all the forest with his delightful voice,
And all praised the young Starling.
Another would be content with such an achievement,
But our Starling heard that they praise the nightingale more,
And was envious.
And he thought: "Wait a moment, friends,
I shall sing even better,
And shall do it with nightingale-like harmony."
And so he began to sing,
But in a most peculiar manner;
Now he squeaked, now he wheezed,
And then he bleated like a young goat;
And in a most unfortunate way,
He yowled like a cat;
In a word, with his singing, he drove away all the birds.
My dear Starling, what did you achieve by that?
It is better to sing well like a goldfinch,
Than badly like a nightingale.

VII
The Pond and the River

"Good Lord," said a Pond to a nearby River,
"Whenever one looks,
Your waters just keep flowing!
Do you really, little sister, not get tired?
Besides that, I often see you carrying
Either heavy-laden vessels or long rafts.
This is not even to mention boats and canoes in great numbers.
When will you give up such a life?
I really would dry up from boredom.
In comparison with you, how pleasant is my fate!
Of course, I am not as grand as you:
On the map I do not stretch across a whole page,
And psaltery-players do not strum praises to me;
But this, really, is all so trivial.
To make up for it, I, against soft and silty banks,
Like a lady in a feather-bed,
Lie both in comfort and in peace;
Not only do I fear neither vessels nor rafts –
I do not even know the weight of a canoe;
Moreover, a leaf barely quivers on my water
When a breeze happens to throw it on me.
What can take the place of such a carefree life?
Sheltered from the winds on all sides,
Motionlessly, I look at worldly bustle
And philosophise as in a dream."
"But, philosophising, do you remember the law of nature,"
The River replied to this,
"That only with movement does water keep fresh?
If I became a great river,

It is because, having renounced the quiet life,
I observe this law.
In return, each year,
Due to the abundance and purity of my water,
I bring benefit, and receive honour and glory.
And I shall, perhaps, still flow for centuries,
When there is no longer a trace of you,
And all talk about you has ceased."
The River's words came true: she flows to this day;
But the poor Pond year after year kept shrinking,
Was all clouded with thick mud,
Grew algae, was overgrown with sedge,
And at last entirely dried up.
In the same way, a gift without benefit to the world fades,
Weakening each day,
When laziness masters it,
And it is not revitalised by activity.

VIII
Trishka's *Kaftan*

Trishka's *kaftan* was worn out at the elbows.
Why spend time thinking? He took up a needle:
He shortened the sleeves by a quarter, and patched the elbows.
The *kaftan* was again ready to wear;
But his arms were now bare by a quarter.
Nothing wrong with that;
However, everyone was laughing at Trishka.
He said: "I really am no fool;
I shall set this matter right:
I shall make the sleeves longer than before."

Oh, Trishka was not incompetent!
He trimmed the back and sides of the *kaftan*,
And lengthened the sleeves. Now Trishka was happy,
Though he wears a *kaftan*
That is even shorter than a jacket.

In such a way I sometimes saw
Other gentlemen,
Who, having ruined their work, try to set it right;
But look closely: they strut around in Trishka's *kaftan*.

IX
The Mechanic

A certain fine fellow bought a huge house,
An old-fashioned house, indeed, but wonderfully well built:
Solidity and comfort – that house had both,
And the house would have pleased him in every way,
Except for just one thing:
It stood rather far from water.
"Well, so what," he thought, "I am the master of my property;
I shall simply arrange to have the house, as it is,
Moved to the river with machines."
(As is evident, the young man was passionate about machines!)
"I have only to put a sledge under it,
Having undermined in advance the foundations,
And then, having also fitted rollers,
Winch the whole building whither I wish,
And set it down as if by hand.
And there will be something else the world has never seen:

When they transfer my house thither,
Accompanied by music, and with friends in the house,
Feasting behind a big table,
To the new location I shall drive as if in a carriage."
Being obsessed by this foolishness,
My Mechanic immediately got down to business.
He hired workers and dug under the house,
Giving no thought for either trouble or expense.
But he was not able to move his house,
And only reached the point
Where the house collapsed.

———————

How many projects do people undertake
That are even more dangerous and foolish than this!

X
The Fire and the Diamond

Having started a conflagration from a little spark,
A Fire spread furiously through buildings
In the quiet midnight hour.
In that general alarm,
A lost Diamond, lying on the road,
Glimmered faintly through the dust.
"How insignificant you are compared to me," said the Fire,
"Despite all your power to glitter!
And what keen eyesight is necessary
In order to distinguish you, even at a short distance,
Either from ordinary glass or from a drop of water,
When either my rays or those of the sun play on them!

So I really do not think it matters if anything happens
to hide you.
Any trifle – a scrap of ribbon, or a single hair winding
around you –
Is able to eclipse your brilliance!
Not so easily is my radiance obscured,
When I, in my fury,
Engulf a building.
Look how all the efforts of people
Against myself I scorn;
How with a roar I devour all that I meet,
And how my glow, reflected in the clouds,
Inspires fear in the neighbourhood!"
"Compared to yours my splendour is indeed poor,"
Replied the Diamond,
"On the other hand, I am harmless:
No one reproaches me with anyone's misfortune,
And my rays are annoying
To jealousy alone;
But you glitter only while you destroy.
And look how, combining all their efforts,
The people strive to extinguish you more quickly.
And the more furiously you blaze,
The closer perhaps you are to your end."
Now, with great exertion, the people got down to
extinguishing the Fire;
The next morning only smoke and stench remained;
But before long the Diamond was discovered,
And was placed in all its radiant beauty in a tsar's crown.

XI
The Hermit and the Bear

Although a good turn to us in time of need is precious,
Not everyone is able to provide it properly.
God forbid that we get involved with a bungler!
An obliging fool is more dangerous than an enemy.

A certain Man lived the solitary life,
Far from town, in the back of beyond.
Write however sweetly you wish about the solitary life;
Still, not everyone is able to live in solitude:
It is comforting for us to share sadness and joy.
You might reply: "But the little meadow, the shaded leafy grove,
The hillocks, little brooks, the lush grass…"
Yes, they are wonderful, it cannot be denied,
But all will become boring when there is no one to talk to.
So even that Hermit grew bored always being alone.
He walked to the woods, to see if there were any neighbours,
So as to make the acquaintance of someone.
But in the woods whom can one meet,
Besides wolves or bears?
And indeed, he met with a big Bear;
There was nothing he could do: he took off his hat
And bowed to the dear neighbour.
The neighbour extended a paw to him
And, little by little, they become acquainted;
Then they became friends,
At last they became inseparable.
Whole days they spent together.

What they had in common, and what conversation took place,
What witticisms or little jokes they shared,
And how their relationship developed,
To this day I do not know.
The Hermit was not talkative,
And bears are by nature taciturn,
So they did not share intimacies about their lives.
However, the Hermit was very happy
That God had given him a treasure in a friend.
He went everywhere behind Misha, and without Misha
pined away;
He could not praise Mishenka highly enough.
Once, on a hot day, the friends bethought themselves
Of wandering for a time, through the groves,
through the meadows,
Up hill and down dale;
But as a man is much weaker than a bear,
So our Hermit grew tired more quickly than Mishenka,
And began to fall behind his friend.
Seeing this, Misha, like a sensible animal, said to the Hermit:
"Do lie down, brother, and rest,
And if you wish, have a nap;
I shall guard you here while you sleep."
The Hermit agreed: he lay down, yawned,
And immediately fell asleep.
Now the Bear, keeping watch, had something to do:
A fly came and sat on his friend's nose: he brushed it off;
He looked – now the fly was on the Hermit's cheek;
He drove it away – then it was on the nose again,
And becoming more persistent with every passing moment.
So our Mishka, not saying a word and barely taking breath,
Lifted a heavy cobblestone in his paws and squatted, thinking:

"Be still, pesky one, I am going to let you have it!"
He lay waiting for the fly to alight on his friend's forehead;
Then, with all his might, he brought the stone down upon it.
The blow was so deft that the skull was split apart,
And Misha's friend remained to lie there a long time.

XII
The Flowers

In the opened window of a rich room,
In painted china pots,
Imitation Flowers, stand next to living ones,
On little wire stems
Swaying haughtily,
Proudly displaying their beauty to all.
Now a light rain began to spit.
The taffeta Flowers appealed to Jupiter,
And begged him to stop the rain;
In every possible way they cursed and vilified the rain.
"Jupiter!" they prayed, "Do stop the rain:
What is the use of it?
What in the world is worse than rain?
Look, it is not even possible to walk along the street:
Everywhere there are only mud and puddles."
But Zeus did not heed the frivolous entreaty,
And the rain duly passed in its own good time.
Having driven away the sultriness,
It cooled the air; the earth sprang to life,
And all of nature was revived.
Then, even in the window, the live Flowers
Spread out in all their beauty,

And became from the rain more fragrant,
Fresher and fuller.
But the poor imitation Flowers, from that time,
Lost all beauty, and were thrown in the yard
Like rubbish.

True talents do not rage against criticism;
It cannot damage their qualities;
Only imitation flowers fear the rain.

XIII
The Peasant and the Snake

A Snake came to a Peasant and asked to be let into the house,
Not to live uselessly, doing nothing –
No, she wanted to look after his children:
Bread is sweeter, if acquired with labour!
"I know," she said,
"The bad reputation that snakes have among you people:
That they are all of most evil disposition.
From ancient times the rumour has gone
That they do not know gratitude;
That they have neither friendships nor blood ties;
That they even eat up their own children.
All this may be so; but I am myself not such.
In my life not only have I never bitten anyone,
But I so abhor evil
That I would allow my fangs to be torn out,
If only I knew that I could live without fangs.
In a word, I am the kindest of snakes.

See for yourself, how I shall love your children!"
"Even if all that were true," said the Peasant,
"I still could not take you in.
If I set such an example, there would crawl in here after you
A hundred evil snakes, and they would kill all my children.
That is why, my dear, to me even the best snake is no good at all,
And it is why I cannot have you live with me."

Friends! Do you understand what I am getting at here?

XIV
The Peasant and the Thief

A Peasant, having acquired a house,
Bought at a trade fair a milk pail and cow,
And with them through a grove
Was quietly trudging home along a dirt track,
When suddenly he encountered a Thief.
The Thief took everything the Peasant had.
"For pity's sake," wailed the Peasant, "I am done for.
You have completely ruined me!
A whole year I saved to buy this cow;
I could hardly wait for this day."
"Very well, then," said the Thief, having been moved to compassion,
"You won't have cause to complain about me.
After all, I really do not milk cows;
So let it be like this:
Keep the pail for yourself."

XV
The Curious Man

"Dear friend, hello. Where have you been?"
"At the exhibition of Curiosities, my friend. I spent three
hours there;
I saw and examined everything.
Believe it or not, I have neither the ability
Nor the strength to tell you of my amazement.
It is indeed true that a palace of wonders is to be found there.
Oh, in creations nature is liberal!
What animals, what birds have I not seen there!
What butterflies, small insects,
Bugs, flies, little cockroaches!
One like emerald, another like coral!
What tiny little ladybirds!
There are, really, some smaller than a pinhead!"
"And did you see the elephant? What a sight it
must have been!
I imagine you thought that you had met a mountain."
"Was an elephant really there?"
"Yes."
"Well, brother, I confess:
I did not see the elephant."

XVI
The Lion Goes Hunting

Once upon a time there lived in the same area
A Dog, a Lion, a Wolf and a Fox.

And here is an agreement they came to
Among themselves:
That they go hunting together,
And whatever they catch, they divide equally among them.
I do not know how, or with what, but I know that at first
The Fox caught a deer,
And sent to her comrades a message,
That they come to share the lucky catch:
Not a bad catch, indeed!
They arrived; the Lion too arrived; he stretched his claws,
And looking around at his comrades,
Prepared to divide the spoil,
And said: " Here we are, friends, all four of us."
And into four pieces he tore the deer.
"Now, let's allocate! Look here, friends:
This here is my part,
According to our agreement;
And this second part, without argument, is due to me as a Lion;
And the third part is mine because I am stronger than any of you.
As for the last part, if any of you so much as extend a paw to it,
That one will not leave this place alive."

XVII

The Horse and Rider

A certain Rider so trained a Horse that,
By hardly even moving the reins,
He got from it everything that he wanted.
The Horse obeyed him with just a word.
"It is pointless even to bridle such a Horse,"
The master said one day,

"Because I have arranged everything to perfection."
Having ridden out to the field, he removed the bridle
from the Horse.
Sensing freedom, the Horse at first only slightly increased speed.
Raising its head and gently shaking its mane,
It went with a playful trot, as if entertaining the Rider.
Then, sensing how weak was the control over it,
The Horse soon gained eagerness from freedom.
Its blood boiled up, its look grew fiery.
Obeying no more the Rider's words,
It rushed him at full tilt across all the wide field.
In vain did my unfortunate Rider,
With trembling hand,
Attempt to put on the bridle:
The Horse only galloped on more furiously.
It finally threw him to the ground,
And set off like a wild whirlwind,
Seeing nothing of the road,
Until it rushed to its death in a ravine.
Now the Rider was grief-stricken.
"My poor steed!" he said, "I am guilty of your end!
Had I not taken off your bridle,
I certainly would have been able to control you:
You would not have thrown me down,
Nor yourself have died so pitiful a death."

However appealing liberty may be,
She is no less disastrous for people,
When she is not given intelligent guidance.

XVIII
The Peasants and the River

Some Peasants, who had lost patience with
brooks and streams
Because of the destruction they had caused by flooding,
Went to ask justice for themselves of the River
Into which those little brooks and streams flowed.
They had much evidence to support their case:
In one place, winter crops had been dug up;
In another, mills torn down and washed away;
Livestock had drowned – so many as to be countless.
The River, however, though mighty, flowed peacefully:
Big towns stood on its banks,
And never had any such complaints about it been heard.
So surely, the Peasants reasoned among themselves,
The River would support them in their dispute
with the streams?
But what happened? When the Peasants drew closer
And looked at the River, they discovered
That it was itself carrying away half their possessions.
Not wishing to complain fruitlessly,
The peasants just stood and gazed at their belongings;
Then, exchanging looks among themselves,
And shaking their heads, they went home.
"We would be wasting our time," they said as they left.
"We shall never bring the weaker ones to justice
As long as they share the spoils equally with
the stronger ones."

XIX
The Kind-hearted Fox

A hunter in spring killed a robin.
That might have been the only misfortune,
But no: three more souls seemed destined to perish after her:
The hunter orphaned three of her poor chicks.
Barely out of the shell, without awareness and without strength,
The little ones suffered from hunger and cold,
And with plaintive squeaks called for their mother in vain.
"How can one not suffer, seeing these little ones.
Whose heart does not ache for them?"
A Fox, sitting on a stone opposite the nest of orphans,
Said to the other birds.
"Dear friends, don't leave the young ones without help.
Each of you bring at least one seed to the poor things;
Each of you place at least one straw in their nest.
In this way will you save their life.
What act of kindness could be more sacred!
Look, Cuckoo, you know you moult a lot;
Would it not be better to allow yourself to be plucked,
So as to line their bed with your feathers?
Otherwise you will just lose those feathers pointlessly.
You, Lark, that atop the summits
Turns somersaults and spins round,
You could search for food in the cornfields and meadows,
And share it with the orphans.
You, Turtle-dove, your chicks are already partly grown,
And would be able to get food for themselves:
So you should abandon your nest,
And sit with the little orphans in place of their mother,

And let God look after your own children.
You, Swallow, could catch midges,
With which to feed the parentless mites.
And you, dear Nightingale –
You know how everyone loves your voice –
You could sing them lullabies,
While the zephyr rocks them in the nest.
Such tenderness, I strongly believe,
Would compensate them for their bitter loss.
Listen to me: we shall show that in the forest
There are kind hearts, and that…"
With these words, all three of the poor little ones,
Not being able, because of hunger, to stay still,
Fell to the Fox beneath.
And what did she do? Immediately ate them,
And did not finish delivering her homily.

Reader, don't be surprised!
He who is sincerely kind does not talk about it,
But does good by stealth;
But the one who just regales others with talk of kindness –
That one often does good only at the expense of others;
Because in that way there is no cost to him whatever.
In this regard almost all such people
Are just like my Fox.

XX
A Community Meeting

Establish whatever rules you like,
But if matters are in the hands of unscrupulous people

> They always find a way
> To do what they want.

A wolf asked the lion if he could be the guardian of the sheep.
With the help of his friend the fox,
A word about it was put in the lioness' ear.
But since wolves have a bad reputation in the world,
And it could not be said
That the lion pays any heed to the encomia of friends,
So all the animal population were ordered
To gather at a general meeting,
And to ask of this one, that one and the other,
What of either good or bad they knew of the wolf.
So the order was carried out: all the animals gathered.
At the gathering all opinions were fittingly voiced,
But against the wolf was heard not a word,
And the wolf was permitted to settle in the sheep-fold.
But what on earth did the sheep have to say?
After all, they were obviously at the meeting?
Not at all! No one had remembered to invite the sheep.
And they were precisely the ones who should
have been asked.

Book Five

I
Demyan's Fish Soup

"Dear neighbour, my friend!
Please, eat."
"My good host, I have had enough."
"No matter, have another plate; listen:
It is a special fish soup, truly, cooked to perfection!"
"I have eaten three bowls of it."
"What, Enough! Why count? If the desire is there,
Or for your health, eat it right up!
What a fish soup! How rich it is,
As if coated in amber.
Do make me happy, dear friend!
Here is some bream, giblets; here are pieces of sterlet!
Just one more spoonful! Come here, wife: entreat our guest!"
Thus did Demyan regale his neighbour Foka,
Giving him neither rest nor peace.
But for a long time the sweat had already been pouring
from Foka's brow.
However, he took one more bowlful,
Summoned the last of his strength, and finished it all.
"Here's a friend I love!" exclaimed Demyan.
"I really cannot tolerate the proud.
Well, now have another bowlful, my dear man!"
At this point my poor Foka,
However much he liked fish soup,

To escape such torment
Took up his hat and sash
And quickly ran home without a glance back;
And he never again set foot in Demyan's house.

Writer, you are fortunate if you have a way with words;
But if you do not know when to be silent,
And if you fail to pity the listening ear,
Then know that your verses and prose
Will be more nauseating than Demyan's fish soup.

II
The Mouse and the Rat

"Dear neighbour! Have you heard the good news?"
A Mouse said to a Rat, having run in.
You know, they say the cat has fallen into the clutches of the lion.
So the time has come for us to rest!"
"Don't rejoice, my dear,"
The Rat said to her in reply,
"And do not hope in vain!
If it comes to a fight between them,
Then I am sure the lion will not come out alive:
There is no beast stronger than a cat!"

How many times have I seen – notice this yourself:
When a coward fears someone,
Then he thinks the whole world
Looks on that person with his eyes.

III
The Siskin and the Pigeon

A vicious trap snared a Siskin;
In it the poor thing was struggling and fluttering about.
Now a young Pigeon noticed, and began to mock her.
"Is it not a shame," he said, "to get caught in broad daylight?
I can confidently assure you
That they would not be able to trick me like that!"
But on the contrary, see what happened:
There and then he himself became entangled in a snare.
Here is the point:
In the future, dear Pigeon, don't laugh at another's misfortune.

IV
The Divers

A certain Tsar in ancient times fell into terrible doubt:
Is there not more harm than benefit in learning?
Are not both the emotions and the will enfeebled by studies?
And would he not act more wisely
If he exiled from the kingdom all learned men?
But since this Tsar, an adornment to his throne,
Was deeply concerned about the happiness of his people,
And for this reason did nothing out of whim or impulse,
So he ordered a council to convene,
In which each member would – not in flowery language,
But sensibly and directly – present his "yes" or "no":
That is, whether learned people should be banned

from the kingdom,
Or allowed to remain as before.
But however the council deliberated –
Some spoke for themselves, others spoke through a secretary –
They all only obscured the matter,
And by their indecision confused the Tsar's mind.
Some said that ignorance is darkness,
That God would not have given us a mind,
Nor a gift to understand spiritual things,
If He wanted Man to understand
No more than do dumb animals;
And that, in view of this,
Knowledge leads people to happiness.
Others maintained
That people only become worse from studies,
That all learning is gibberish,
That from it comes only harm to nature,
And that it was because of education
That the most powerful kingdoms in the world fell.
In short: with both sides spouting both sense and nonsense,
The council covered mountains of paper,
But came to no conclusions on the subject of learning.
The Tsar did more.
He summoned to a convention clever men from everywhere,
And directed them to settle the matter.
But even this method was bad,
Because the Tsar paid them handsomely;
And so, for them, disagreement in opinion was a gold mine;
And if he had given them free rein
They would to this day be deliberating –
And taking their salaries.
Realising this, he quickly dismissed them,

The Fables of Ivan Krylov

For the Tsar kept a watchful eye on the Treasury.
Meanwhile, with every passing day, he fell into more doubt.
Then one day, occupied with these thoughts,
He walked out and saw before him a hermit
With a grey beard and with a big book in his hands.
The hermit had a look that was solemn, but not grim:
A smile of cordiality and kindness adorned his mouth,
And on his brow were visible traces of deep thought.
The monarch entered into conversation with the hermit
And, seeing in him boundless knowledge,
Asked that wise man to settle the important debate:
Is learning beneficial, or harmful?
"Tsar!" the old man replied, "allow me,
By means of a simple parable,
To tell you what many years meditation have revealed to me."
Having collected his thoughts, the hermit began thus:
"On the seashore,
In India lived a fisherman;
Having led a long life of poverty and sorrow,
He died leaving three sons.
But the boys,
Seeing that they could barely make a living from fishing,
And moreover hating the paternal trade,
Thought to take from the sea a richer gift:
Not fish, but pearls.
Knowing how to swim and dive,
They set out to extract from the sea what it owed them.
However, success was different for all three:
One, lazier than the others,
Just wandered along the shore;
He did not even want to wet his legs,
And only waited for those pearls

That were thrown to him by a wave;
But, with such laziness, he just barely scraped a living.
Another, not sparing labour in the least,
And knowing the depth to which he could descend,
Dived to seek rich pearls at the bottom,
Becoming richer by the day.
But the third, tortured by greed for riches,
Reasoned thus with himself:
'Though it may be possible to find pearls near the shore,
What treasures should I not expect to find
Were I able to reach the very bottom of the sea?
There may be countless riches there,
Mountains of corals, pearls and precious stones,
Which I shall only have to reach out for and grasp.'
Being fascinated by this thought,
The madman soon set out for the open sea
And, having chosen the greatest depth,
Threw himself into the abyss – and was drowned.
Because of arrogance, without reaching the bottom,
He paid with his life.
Oh Tsar!" the sage now added,
"Though in learning we find the source of many blessings,
The rash mind discovers in it an abyss and a disastrous end;
But with this difference:
That often in his destruction he drags down others with him."

V

The Mistress and Two Maids

A Lady, an old woman, finicky,
Indefatigable and peevish,

Had two girls, Maids,
Whose duty was from morning even until deepest night
Unceasingly to spin.
For the girls it was unbearable;
For them, work days and holidays were all the same;
The old Lady gave them no peace.
By day she allowed them no break from weaving.
At dawn, while others were still asleep,
Their spindle had already long been dancing.
Perhaps sometimes the old Lady would have been late,
But in that house there was a damned cockerel:
As soon as it began to crow, the old Lady would rise,
Throw on a fur jacket and cap,
Fan the embers in the stove
And trudge along, muttering, to the spinners' bedroom.
She would shake them with a bony hand
And, if they turned obstinate, beat them with her walking stick,
Disturbing their sweet sleep in the dawn.
What could be done with her?
The poor girls would grimace, yawn, huddle up,
And reluctantly part company with their warm bed.
The next day again, just as the cockerel raised a cry,
The girls would have from the mistress the same treatment:
They would be woken up and put to work on the loom.
"All right, you malignant creature!"
The spinners muttered through their teeth at the cock,
"Without your songs we surely would get more sleep;
You really are the one to blame!"
And, having found an opportunity,
Without pity the Girls wrung the cockerel's neck.
But what happened? In this way they expected relief,
But in fact the matter turned out quite differently.

It was true, the cockerel no longer sang –
The villain was no more –
But the Mistress, in order that no time be lost,
Barely allowed the Girls to close their eyes after they lay down
Before she began to awaken them each day
Earlier than the cock had ever crowed.
Now, too late, the Girls understood
That they had fallen from the fire into the flame.

So, wishing to get out of trouble,
Often people have the same fate:
No sooner do they eliminate one woe
Than – look! – they acquire another worse.

VI

The Stone and the Worm

"What a disturbance has it caused here! What a boor!"
Said a Stone – which was lying in a field – about the rain.
"I daresay everyone is glad about it – look!
They waited for it as for a dear guest,
But what on earth did it do?
It only went on for two or three hours.
People should ask about me!
I have been here for ages: quiet, always modest,
I lie very contentedly wherever they throw me,
And never receive thanks.
For good reason, indeed, is the world criticised:
I see no justice at all in it."
"Silence!" Said a Worm to him.

"This rain, however short a time it lasted,
Abundantly watered the field,
Which had been deprived of its life by drought,
And revived hope for farmers.
But you are merely a useless burden on the land."

Thus boasts another, who serves forty years
But, like the Stone, benefits no one.

VII
The Bear and the Hives

Once, in spring-time, Mishka the Bear
Was chosen by the other animals to oversee the hives.
Now, it is known that bears have a weakness for honey,
So they might have chosen a more appropriate guardian:
Then there would have been no concern.
Well, you ask for sense in animals!
Of those who applied for the position,
All were sent away disappointed
And, as if as a joke,
Mishka found himself appointed.
In the end, sin resulted:
My Mishka began to take all the honey to his lair.
This was discovered; the alarm was raised
And, following due procedure, a court was convened,
Which sent Mishka into retirement, and ordered
That the old rogue spend the whole winter in his cave.
So the matter was settled, finished, ratified;
But they never recovered the honey.

Mishka didn't care:
He bid farewell to the world,
Got into his warm lair,
And there licked the honey from his paws,
And waited for the scandal to blow over.

VIII

The Mirror and the Monkey

A Monkey, seeing her reflection in a mirror,
Gently nudged a bear with her foot:
"Do look," she said, "my good friend:
What an ugly mug is that!
What grimaces and twitches it has!
I would hang myself from grief
If I resembled it even a little.
But you know, it must be said, there are
Among my relatives five or six such eyesores;
I can even count them on my fingers."
"Rather than labour to count your relatives,"
The bear replied,
"Would it not be better to think of yourself, my friend?"
But the bear's advice went unheeded.

There are many examples like this in the world:
No one likes to recognise himself in criticism.
I saw that just yesterday:
Everyone knows that Klimich is dishonest;
They lecture him about taking bribes,
But he craftily blames Pyotr.

IX
The Mosquito and the Shepherd

A Shepherd was sleeping in the shade, relying on his dogs.
Seeing this, a snake from under the bushes,
Thrusting out her fangs, crawled to him;
The Shepherd would have been no longer for this world,
Except that a Mosquito, taking pity on him,
With all its might bit the sleeping man.
Waking up, the Shepherd killed the snake;
But first, the half-asleep man so struck the Mosquito
That the poor thing was flattened.

Of such examples there are not a few:
If the weak, moved by kindness,
Attempt to open the eyes of the strong to the truth,
One expects the same to happen to them
As happened to the Mosquito.

X
The Peasant and Death

Having gathered fallen branches in the cold winter time,
An old man, all withered from poverty and labour,
Was slowly dragging himself home to his smokey little hovel,
Groaning and moaning under a heavy load of firewood.
He seemed to be carrying it for ever, and grew tired;
He stopped.

Lowering the firewood to the ground from his shoulders,
He sat down on it, sighed and thought to himself:
"My God! How poor I am.
I am in need of everything; in addition I have a wife
and children;
Then there is the poll tax, land tax, quitrent…
And when in my life have I ever had
Even a single joyful day?
Amid such despondency, cursing his fate,
He called upon Death.
We have Death never far away:
She is often just behind our back.
She appeared in an instant,
And said: "Why did you call me, old man?"
Seeing her fierce look, the poor man
Was struck dumb and barely able to utter,
"I called you, not at all in anger,
But to ask you to help me lift my bundle."

―――――――

From this fable
We are able to see that,
However hard it is to live,
To die is yet more difficult.

XI
The Knight

A certain Knight in olden times,
Who had conceived the idea of seeking great adventures,
Prepared for war

Against sorcerers and ghosts;
He put on armour and ordered his horse to be brought
to the porch.
But first, rather than sit in the saddle,
He considered it his duty to appeal to the horse with this speech:
"Listen, my eager and faithful steed:
Race across the fields, over the mountains, through forests,
Whither your eyes lead,
As the knight's code commands,
And look for the road to the temple of glory!
When I have conquered all evil spirits,
I shall get in matrimony a Chinese princess,
And shall subdue two or three kingdoms.
Then your labours, my friend, I shall not forget:
I shall share all the glory with you.
A stable, like a huge palace,
I shall arrange to be built for you;
And in summer I shall lead you out to the water meadows.
Now you are little acquainted even with oats,
But then shall there be for us an abundance of all:
Barley will be your fodder, sweet indeed your swill."
Here the Knight jumped into the saddle and took up the reins.
But his horse was having none of it,
And trotted directly back to its stall.

XII
A Man and his Shadow

A certain scatter-brained Man wanted to try and catch
his Shadow:
He walked to her, but she went on ahead; he hastened his step,

But still she stayed in front; finally, he began to run;
But the more quickly he ran, the faster ran his Shadow,
Like treasure not letting herself be caught.
Now my poor Fool suddenly turned back.
He glanced behind,
But his Shadow had already begun to pursue him.

Young ladies! Many times have I heard…
What do you think? But no – this fable is not about you;
It is often what is true about our fortune.
One person spends time and effort in vain,
Trying with all his strength to overtake her;
Another, as it seems, runs entirely away from her:
But that is precisely the one she herself likes to chase.

XIII
The Peasant and the Axe

A Peasant building a hut grew angry with his Axe:
He thought the Axe a poor tool, and went into a rage:
He himself was incompetent,
But the Axe was guilty of everything,
And the Peasant somehow always found a reason to scold it.
"Good for nothing!" he cried once.
"From now on I shall just use you to trim stakes,
While I, with my skill and determination,
And what is more, not begrudging the time,
Shall finish the task.
Know that I am able to get along without you,
And shall make with a simple knife,

What another cannot build even with an axe."
"I shall chop as you command, such is my fate,"
Humbly replied the Axe to the angry outburst.
"If that, my master, is your sacred will,
Then I am ready to serve you in every possible way;
But just be careful that you do not live to regret it:
You will blunt me to no purpose,
But with a knife you will never build a hut."

XIV

The Lion and the Wolf

While a Lion was eating a lamb for breakfast,
A little dog,
Hanging around the Tsar's table,
From under the Lion's claws, grabbed a little piece;
The king of beasts tolerated this with equanimity:
The dog was still young and ignorant.
Seeing this, the thought occurred to a Wolf
That the Lion, if so meek, could not be strong:
So he also extended a paw to the lamb.
But the result for the Wolf was bad:
He himself fell victim to the Lion.
The Lion tore him to pieces, saying:
"Friend, mistakenly, looking at the little dog,
Did you think that towards you too I would be indulgent:
But she is still young and inexperienced,
While you ought to know better."

XV
The Dog, Man, Cat and Falcon

A Dog, a Man, a Cat and a Falcon
Once pledged eternal friendship to one another –
Friendship genuine, sincere, wholehearted.
They shared a house and ate much the same sort of food.
They vowed to divide even joy and trouble,
To help one another,
To stand up for one another
And, if necessary, to die for one another.
So once, having all set out together to hunt,
The friends strayed far from home.
They grew tired, and stopped by a stream to rest.
Here they all started to doze, some lying, some even sitting,
When suddenly a bear, mouth gaping,
Lumbered out at them from the woods.
Seeing such a terrifying sight,
The Falcon rose into the air and the Cat ran off to the forest.
The Man here would have bidden farewell to life;
But the faithful Hound
Threw himself into combat with the evil beast:
He seized hold of the bear,
And no matter how brutally the bear mauled him,
No matter how loudly the bear roared with pain and fury,
The Hound, having bitten through to the bone,
Hung on and did not release his teeth
Until he lost all strength – and life itself.
And the Man? For shame,
None of us compares in faithfulness with a dog:
While the bear was occupied in fight,

He, having picked up his rifle,
With all haste set off home.

We talk glibly of kindness and help,
But only in time of need do we recognise the true friend.
How rare are such friends!
And I must say, how often have I seen,
Just as in this fable the true Hound was abandoned,
So, that one,
Who from trouble was by a friend delivered,
Abandons him in misfortune
And abuses him everywhere.

XVI
Gout and the Spider

Hell itself sent into the world both Gout and the Spider.
This belief La Fontaine spread through all the world.
I shall not start to weigh and measure, after him,
How much truth is here, and why;
And besides, it seems, you can believe his fables
Only if you do not analyse them too closely.
And so it happened, no doubt about it,
That hell gave birth to both Gout and the Spider.
When they had grown up, and the time arrived
To settle them in positions
(For a concerned father, grown-up children are a burden,
Until they are settled!)
Then, releasing them into the world,
The parent said to them: "Go,

You dear children, into the world, and divide it
between you!
There is great potential in you,
And I hope that there you both will uphold my honour,
And both equally pester people.
So decide: from now on
What destiny each of you will take.
There: do you see magnificent houses?
And over there: squalid shacks?
In the first are freedom, prosperity, beauty;
In the others, cramped and crowded conditions,
Hard labour, and poverty."
"There is no reason at all for me to live in a shack,"
Said the Spider. "As for me," said Gout,
"I do not need a palace. Let my brother live in them.
In a village, far away from pharmacies, I am happy to live;
Otherwise there will be doctors,
To chase me away from each rich house."
Reaching agreement, brother and sister appeared in the world.
In the most splendid mansion
The Spider marked out ownership for himself:
Along luxuriant, embroidered damask,
And along gilded cornices
He laid out a web;
And he would have picked up flies in abundance;
But by dawn, with his work barely accomplished,
A servant appeared and with a brush swept everything away.
My Spider was patient: he moved to the stove.
But from there with a broom was swept away.
Hither, thither, the Spider, my poor little thing, was moved;
But wherever he stretched his web,
Either the brush or the duster found him,

And tore all his work to shreds,
While quite often also sweeping him away.
The Spider, in despair, went out of town
To meet his little sister.
"Maybe in villages," he said, "she lives like a queen."
He arrived – but the poor sister in the peasant's hut
Was more miserable than any spider in the world:
With her, the master still mowed hay,
And chopped and carried firewood:
It is a sign of humble people,
That the more they torment gout with labour,
The sooner they are rid of it.
"No, brother," she said, "there is no life for me in the field!"
But her brother was glad about that;
He there and then exchanged lots with her:
He crawled into the peasant's hut, investigated the place,
And, fearing neither the brush nor the broom,
Spread webs all over the ceiling, walls and corners.
As for Gout – she immediately set off on the road,
Said goodbye to the village,
Arrived in the capital, and in the most splendid quarters
Lodged herself in the foot of a grey-haired excellency.
Paradise for the Gout! Life went from the old man:
Together with him she did not even get out of bed.
From that time on, brother and sister no longer met;
They remained in their own environment,
Equally contented with their lot:
The Spider set off to peasants in their hovels,
The Gout – to men of distinction;
And both did wisely.

XVII
The Lion and the Fox

A Fox, never having seen in her life a Lion,
On meeting one almost expired from fear.
Then, a little later, again she came across the Lion;
But now he did not appear to her so terrible.
Then, the third time,
She even entered into conversation with the Lion.

In the same way we also fear the unknown –
Until we get used to it.

XVIII
The Hop

A Hop came out in a kitchen garden
And suddenly began to twine around a dry stake.
In a field nearby was growing a young oak.
"What use is there in that freak,"
The Hop complained to the stake about the oak,
"And indeed in all of his kind?
How does he compare with you?
You are a lady compared to him by virtue of your straightness.
Though he is dressed indeed with leaves,
What rough bark he has, what dull colouring!
Why does the earth support him?"

Not even a week had passed after this
Before the master of the house broke the stake into firewood,
And transplanted the little oak to the kitchen garden.
His labour was rewarded with success:
The little oak took root and put forth branches;
But just look: around it my Hop had already begun to wind,
And to heap honour and praise on that oak.

Such is the behaviour of the flatterer:
He talks a heap of lies and nonsense about you.
But pay no attention to this.
You may not be among his favourites,
But as soon as he falls on hard times
He will be the first to come calling.

XIX
The Elephant in Favour

An Elephant once found favour in the eyes of a lion.
In an instant gossip went through the woods about this.
And so, as usually happens, began the guesswork:
How did the Elephant insinuate himself into favour?
It is not as if elephants are handsome, or amusing;
Just look at their appearance, and at how they walk!
The animals talked among themselves.
"If," said the fox, swishing her tail,
"He had such a fluffy tail, I would not be surprised."
"Or, little sister," said the bear, "at least if he had claws,
He would have been favoured:
No one would have thought that extraordinary;

But it is commonly known that he does not even have claws."
Now the ox entered into the conversation.
"Did he not find favour because of his tusks?
Could they not be considered as horns?"
"So you do not know," said the ass, flapping his ears,
"How he was able to catch the lion's fancy,
And be appointed to high rank.
But I have guessed the reason:
Without long ears he would never have enjoyed preferment.

Although we do not notice it, by praising others
Quite often we eagerly honour ourselves.

XX
The Storm-Cloud

Over land exhausted from intense heat,
A great Storm-Cloud went scudding past.
Leaving not a single drop to revive the earth,
She shed a heavy rain over the sea,
And of her generosity boasted to the mountain.
But the mountain replied to her:
"What good have you done with such generosity?"
And how painful it is to look on.
Had you spilled your rain on the fields,
You would have saved the whole region from famine;
But in the sea, without you, my friend, there is water enough."

XXI
The Slanderer and the Snake

Mistakenly does the world say about demons
That they know nothing at all of justice.
In truth, their judgments are quite often sound.
I shall give an example of that here.
Once upon a time, in hell,
A Snake was walking with a Slanderer in
ceremonial procession.
Neither wanted to cede first place to the other,
And so began a quarrel,
About which of them had the right to walk in front.
Now, it is well known that in hell priority is given
To the one who has caused greatest trouble to those around.
So in this heated and considerable argument
The Slanderer exhibited his tongue to the Snake,
While to him the Snake boasted of her sting.
She hissed, that she could not endure an insult,
And tried hard to crawl ahead of him.
Now the Slanderer would have found himself falling behind,
But Beelzebub intervened:
All credit to him, he stood up for the Slanderer,
And forced back the Snake, saying:
"Though I recognise your achievements,
I must render first place to him:
You are evil – your sting is fatal;
You are dangerous, when near;
You sting without reason (and that is good enough!)
But can you sting from such a distance
As the evil tongue of the Slanderer,

From whom it is not possible to find refuge
Either behind the mountains or beyond the seas?
Therefore it stands to reason that he is more harmful than you:
So crawl behind him, and be in the future more humble."
Since that time,
Slanderers in hell have been more honoured than snakes.

XXII
Fortune and the Beggar

With a worn and decrepit bag,
A destitute Beggar was loitering beneath the windows
Of a grand house and lamenting his fate.
He was often surprised at how
People living in rich dwellings,
Up to the ears in gold, enjoying ease and prosperity,
Were still dissatisfied,
However full their pockets were stuffed.
This, even to the point where,
Senselessly craving and acquiring new riches,
They quite often lost everything they had.
Here, for example, the former master of this house
Had gone successfully into trade,
And had sold all his goods.
At that point it would have been better to stop,
And quietly live out the rest of his days,
Leaving his business to another.
But in the spring he sent more ships to sea;
He expected mountains of gold; but the ships broke up;
The sea absorbed all his treasures;
Now they are at the bottom,

And he sees himself as a rich man only in his dreams.
Another set out in farming,
And very nearly became a millionaire.
But it was not enough: he wanted to double his money.
He overextended himself and was completely ruined.
In short, there are thousands of such examples;
And it serves them right: know when to stop!
Now, suddenly, Fortune appeared to the Pauper
And said to him:
"Listen, for a long time have I desired to help you;
I have found a pile of gold coins;
Put your bag under my hands: I shall fill it –
But only on one condition:
Although everything that falls into the bag will be gold,
If any of it drops from the bag on to the floor,
It will turn to dust.
Be careful: I have warned you in advance:
I am ordered to keep strictly to that condition;
Your bag is old; don't be greedy;
Ensure that it will hold all that you take."
My Beggar could hardly breathe from joy,
And barely noticed the ground under his feet.
He spread his bag; and with a generous hand
There poured into it a golden rain of coins.
The bag soon became heavy.
"Is it enough?" asked Fortune.
"Not yet." – "I hope the bag doesn't burst." – "Don't worry."
"Look, you are already as rich as Croesus."
"More, a little bit more: add just another handful."
"Oh, it's enough! Look, the bag is starting to spread."
"A little pinch more…"
But here the bag burst.

The treasure spilled out and turned to dust.
Fortune stole away: only the bag remained;
And the Beggar was left as poor as ever.

XXIII
The Frog and Jupiter

Living in a swamp at the foot of a mountain,
A Frog in spring moved up the slope.
She found there a muddy place in a hollow,
And set up home. It was like a little paradise,
Under a bush, in the shade, among grasses.
But she did not enjoy it for long.
Summer set in, and with it the heat,
And the Croaker's summer residence became so dry
That flies could roam in it without wetting their legs.
"Oh, you gods!" prayed the Frog from her hole,
"Don't let me, a poor one, perish!
Flood the ground to the height of the mountain top,
So that the water in my estate would never dry up!"
The frog wailed unceasingly,
Until Jupiter finally lost patience, saying that there was,
In her complaint, neither compassion nor sense.
"Stupid one!" Jupiter said,
(But on this occasion I do not think he was really angry),
"You croak to no purpose.
Rather than have me drown all people
For the sake of your foolish scheme,
Would it not be better for you to return to the swamp?"

In life we find many such people,
Who care for no one but themselves,
And who think, if only they are all right,
Then the rest of the world can go to hell.

XXIV
The Fox-Builder

A certain lion was a great lover of hens;
But they did badly at his place.
And this was not really surprising:
Their enclosure was insecure,
So either they were stolen
Or they themselves wandered off.
In order to prevent further loss and grief,
The lion bethought himself of building a big hen house,
And to design it so cunningly, and to set it up so well,
That it would be a deterrent to thieves,
While being for the hens both comfortable and spacious.
Now the lion was informed that the Fox
Was a great master at building,
So he entrusted the project to her;
It was started and finished successfully:
The Fox had applied to it all her effort and skill.
All who looked said the enclosure was a lovely sight.
And moreover everything was there – whatever
was wanted:
Food was under the nose, roosts were placed everywhere;
There was refuge from the cold and the heat,
And little sheltered corners for the brood-hens.
All glory and honour to our dear Fox!

Rich reward was given to her,
And immediately the order was issued,
That the hens were to occupy their house without delay.
But was the change an improvement?
No: though the yard seemed secure enough –
For the fence was strong and high –
With every passing day the number of hens declined.
No one could imagine why this was happening,
So the lion ordered the mounting of a guard.
Who was caught? The very same Fox, the scoundrel.
Though she had indeed designed the house
In such a way that no one could get in,
She had nevertheless left a little hole for herself.

XXV
The Wrongful Accusation

How often, having done something wrong,
Do we place the blame for it on another?
And how often do we say:
"Had it not been for him, it would not have occurred to me!"
And if there are no people to blame,
Then the devil himself is guilty,
Though he hadn't been there at all.
Of this there are a multitude of examples. Here is one:
In an Eastern country once there lived a Brahmin who,
Though professing to be of sincere faith,
Was not such in the conduct of his life.
(Even among Brahmins there are hypocrites;
but this is an aside):
The point is simply that

He was the only one of that kind in his brotherhood:
All the others led lives of saintliness.
What to him was most tiresome of all,
Was that their superior was of disposition most severe,
So that no one in any way dared to transgress the rules.
However, my Brahmin was not thwarted.
A fast-day came, and he wondered
If it would be possible to indulge in feast-foods in secret.
He got an egg, waited for midnight
And, having lit a candle,
On this candle set about to cook the egg.
He turned it gently over the flame;
Not averting his eyes, he swallowed it mentally.
And about his superior he reflected, laughing:
"You certainly will not catch me,
My long-bearded friend!
I shall eat this egg with the greatest pleasure."
But in fact there now suddenly and quietly appeared
To the Brahmin in his cell his superior,
Who, seeing such sin,
Sternly demanded an explanation.
The evidence was plain, impossible to deny!
"Forgive me holy father,"
The Brahmin begged through his tears.
"Forgive my transgression!
I myself do not know how I fell into temptation;
Ah, a cursed demon incited me!"
But now, suddenly, a little devil, from behind the stove,
Cried: "Shame on you, for always blaming us!
I myself have just this very hour learned from you,
And indeed see for the first time,
How to cook an egg over a candle."

XXVI
Fortune Comes to Visit

We are generous in reproaching Fortune.
Some are not high-ranking, others are not rich;
But for everything and about everything they blame Fortune.
But look carefully: you will see that they themselves
are responsible.
Fortune is blind, roaming among people,
And does not visit only grandees and tsars:
She can be found even in your humble abode.
Perhaps, sometimes, it suits her to stay for awhile:
But do not lose so much as a moment
When she looks in on you;
If you value her, a single minute with her
Will reward years of patience.
But if you do not profit when Fortune calls,
Then not Fortune, but you yourself are to blame;
And be assured, she may not return for an age.

A miserable old hut stood on the edge of town;
Three brothers lived in it, and could not get rich:
Somehow, for them, nothing succeeded.
Whatever any of them undertook,
It all came to nothing.
Everywhere there was either an obstacle or a loss;
According to them, Fortune was responsible for this.
Then, invisible to them, Fortune dropped in.
Having been touched by their great poverty,
She decided wholeheartedly to help them

In whatever enterprises they undertook,
And to stay with them all summer long.
All summer: can you believe it!
The three paupers' affairs all went in different ways.
Although one of them was a failure as a small-tradesman,
Now, whatever he sold, whatever he bought,
He squeezed out a big profit on everything.
He never suffered a loss,
And soon became as rich as Croesus.
Another became an administrator: at any other time
He might have remained in a lowly clerical position,
But now success came to him from all directions.
Whether he gave a dinner, or obsequiously
welcomed dignitaries,
He was rewarded with either rank or a grant of land.
Look: he soon owned a house, and a country place,
and a village.
Now you will ask: what did the third receive?
After all, Fortune probably helped him as well?
Of course: with him she hardly rested.
But the third brother spent the whole summer catching flies,
And was so successful that it was amazing!
I do not know whether he was good at that before;
But now his labours were richly rewarded:
Whenever he waved his hand, thanks to Fortune,
Not once did he fail to kill a fly.
And so the Guest finished her long stay with the brothers,
And set off further on the way,
Leaving two brothers in profit: one of them rich,
another in rank;
But the third brother cursed his fate,
That evil Fortune had left him a beggar.

Reader, be yourself the judge.
Who really was to blame for this?

Book Six

I
The Wolf and the Shepherds

A Wolf, circling around a Shepherd's yard,
And seeing through the fence that,
Having selected the best rams in the flock,
The Shepherds were calmly slaughtering them
While their dogs lay quietly nearby,
Said to himself in annoyance as he went away:
"What a hue and cry would you all raise here, friends,
If I were to do the same."

II
The Cuckoo and the Turtle-Dove

A Cuckoo on a bough was sadly calling.
"Why, my friend, are you so sad?"
Tenderly cooed a Dove to her from a branch.
"Is it because spring has passed, and with it, love;
And because the sun has descended lower,
Bringing us closer to winter?"
"How should I, a poor one, not grieve?"
Said the Cuckoo. "You yourself be the judge:
I was happily in love this spring,
And at last I became a mother;
But the children do not at all want to know me.

Did I expect such recompense from them?
And do I not feel envious when I see
How ducklings cling to their mother,
How the chicks gather like drops of rain at her call,
While I, like an orphan, sit entirely alone,
Knowing nothing of the affection of children?"
"Poor thing! I sincerely pity you.
The indifference of children would be enough to kill me,
Though such cases are not unusual.
But tell me: have you already raised children?
When were you able to build a nest?
I really did not see this happening.
You kept soaring, and gliding, and swooping."
"It would have been silly of me," said the Cuckoo,
"To waste so many fine days sitting in a nest.
That would have been the stupidest thing of all!
No: I always laid my eggs in the nests of others."
"Then what affection," the Turtle-dove replied,
"Can you expect from your children?"

Fathers and Mothers! The lesson of this fable is for you.
I have told it not as an excuse for bad children:
Disrespect in them toward their parents,
Like ingratitude, is always a sin.
But if they grow up separated from you,
And entrusted to mercenary hands,
Then are you yourselves not guilty
If in your old age they are little consolation to you?

III
The Comb

A mother, to groom the head of her child,
Bought a fine-toothed little Comb.
The child refused to part with it:
Whether he was playing, or learning a lesson from his primer,
He kept admiring it,
And with it combing his golden curls –
Wavy, like a lamb's, and soft, like fine flax.
And what a Comb it was! Not only did it not pull –
Nowhere did it even get caught in his hair,
But ran smooth and straight.
In the eyes of the boy it was priceless.
Then one day it happened that the Comb was lost.
The boy began to run and play,
And his shock of hair became dishevelled.
His nanny tried to tend his hair, but he raised a howl:
"Where is my comb?"
So the comb was found;
But his hair was just too matted for the Comb,
Which pulled painfully, driving him nearly to tears.
"How wicked you are, you bad Comb!"
Cried the boy.
But the Comb replied: "My friend, I am the same as before;
It is your hair that is now too unkempt to be managed."
But the boy, from anger and vexation,
Threw the Comb in the river,
Where now it is used by the Naiads.

I have seen in my time
That people treat truth just the same:
While their conscience is clear,
Truth to them is dear and sacred;
They listen to and accept her;
But if their conscience is not clear,
Then they distance themselves from the truth;
And they all become like a child
That does not want to comb dishevelled hair.

IV

The Miser and the Hen

A miser loses everything, hoping to get all.
One need not seek long for examples:
There are many of them: I know this to be so.
But I am too lazy to go looking, so I intend
To tell you an old fable.

This is what in childhood I read about a Miser.
He was a man
Who knew no trade or profession whatever,
But his coffers grew visibly stout.
He had a Hen (how enviable this is!)
Who laid eggs,
And not ordinary eggs,
But golden eggs.
Another would be glad enough,
That little by little he was becoming rich;
But this was not true of the Miser:

The thought occurred to him
That if he cut open the Hen he would find treasure inside.
And so, forgetting her generosity to him,
And not fearing the sin of ingratitude,
He slaughtered her.
But what happened?
As a reward, he pulled from her just ordinary giblets.

V

The Two Barrels

Two Barrels were rolling downhill:
One was filled with wine,
The other was empty.
The first rolled quietly, ponderously;
The other bounced along at speed,
Banging and crashing on the road,
And raising a column of dust.
A passer-by nimbly and fearfully moved aside,
Having heard it coming from afar.
But however loud that Barrel was,
It was of less worth than the other.

―――――――――

In those who incessantly shout about their doings
There is probably little of value;
True achievers are often those of few words.
Successful people are loud only in deeds,
And think important thoughts
Without making a noise.

VI
Alcides

Alcides, son of Alcmena,
So renowned for courage and miraculous strength,
Once, passing along a dangerous path
Between a cliff and a precipice,
Saw on the path a thing
Barely visible lying curled up, like a hedgehog.
What it was, he did not know.
His impulse was to crush it under his heel. So what happened?
It swelled and became more than twice the size.
His anger having flared up, Alcides now
Struck it with his heavy cudgel.
But he saw
That it only assumed a look more terrible:
It grew bigger, swelled and became huge;
It blocked the light of the sun,
And obscured all the path for Alcides.
He dropped the cudgel and before this wondrous object
Grew motionless with astonishment.
Then to him Athena suddenly appeared.
"Abandon this useless contest, my brother!" she said.
"The name of this monster is Discord.
If it is not disturbed, one barely notices it;
But no one should think to fight with it:
From quarrels it only becomes bigger,
And grows higher than a mountain."

VII
Apelles and the Ass' Foal

One possessed of immoderate self-esteem,
Is proud even of that which others find ridiculous in him;
And he often comes to boast of that
Of which he should be ashamed.

———————

Meeting with an Ass' Foal,
Apelles invited the young Ass to visit him;
The very bones of the Foal began to shake with excitement.
He perfumed all the forest with his boasting,
Saying to the animals: "How tiresome Apelles is to me,
Whenever I meet him he keeps pestering me,
And inviting me to visit him.
It seems to me, my friends,
That he intends to use me as a model for Pegasus.
"No," said Apelles, who happened to be near,
"I intend to draw the court of Midas,
And wanted to use your ears as a model for his.
If you would like to visit me, I should be pleased to see you.
Though I have seen many asses' ears,
Those of a size such as yours
I have never before seen –
Either on foals or even on full-grown beasts.

VIII
The Hunter

How often in life do people say: I can do it later.
But one has to admit

That those who say this are not acting rationally,
But succumbing to laziness.
Therefore, if there is business to do, finish it quickly,
Or afterwards blame only yourself, not fortune,
If the unexpected catches you unawares.
I shall do my best to show you this in a fable.

A Hunter, having taken his rifle, ammunition, a bag
And faithful friend Hector,
Went to the woods to hunt, as was his custom.
His rifle was unloaded,
Though he had been advised to load it at home.
"What nonsense!" he said. "I know the road:
On it I have never seen so much as a sparrow;
It is a whole hour's walk up to where the game is found,
So I shall have a hundred opportunities to load."
But what happened? He had barely stepped out of the house
(It was as if fortune were playing a trick on him)
When he saw a whole flock of ducks on the little lake.
Our Rifleman would easily have been able to kill
About a dozen with a single cartridge,
And to have food for a week,
Had he not delayed loading the rifle.
Now he quickly reached for a cartridge;
But the ducks sensed this:
While he busied himself with the rifle,
They were roused, gave a screech,
Rose up and – flew off in formation beyond the woods;
And there they hid themselves from view.
In vain then did the rifleman trudge through the forest,
Not coming across so much as a sparrow.

And now to one misfortune was added another:
Bad weather set in.
And so my Hunter
Arrived home drenched to the skin,
And with an empty bag.
But still he did not blame himself – he blamed bad luck.

IX
The Boy and the Snake

A Boy, thinking to catch an eel,
Grabbed a Snake and, having seen what he had done,
From fear went as white as his shirt.
The Snake, looking calmly at the Boy, said:
"Listen, if from now on you are not more careful,
Then your recklessness will not be so easily overlooked.
This time God will pardon you; but beware in the future,
And know with whom you trifle!"

X
The Swimmer and the Sea

Having been thrown on the shore by a boiling wave,
A Swimmer from exhaustion sank into a heavy sleep;
Then, on awakening, he started to curse the Sea.
"You," he said, "are guilty of everything!
Being so alluring, you attract us
With your cunning stillness to come to you;
And, having attracted us, you drown us in your depths."
Here the Sea, taking on the aspect of Amphitrite,

Said to the Swimmer:
"Why do you blame me so unjustly?
To swim in my waters is neither frightening nor dangerous;
When the ocean depths rage,
Only Aeolus deserves to be blamed:
He gives me at such times no peace.
If you do not believe me, then see this for yourself:
When the winds are asleep, send ships;
Then shall I be more motionless than the Earth."

And I say, the advice was good:
It is impossible to voyage under sail without wind.

XI
The Donkey and the Peasant

A Peasant in summer acquired a Donkey
To chase away from the kitchen garden
Impudent families of crows and sparrows.
The Donkey was of most honest principles,
Acquainted with neither greed nor theft;
He did not eat a single leaf of the master's
And, I regret to say, he gave the birds a hard life.
But the Peasant profited little from the garden.
The Donkey, in order to chase off the birds,
Galloped far and wide at such speed along all the beds
That everything in the garden was trampled and crushed.
Seeing that his labour had been wasted,
The Peasant retaliated for his loss
By applying a cudgel to the Donkey's back.

"So what!" all might cry. "It served the beast right!
Was it sensible for him
To take on this duty?"

And I would add, not in order to take the Donkey's part,
For he certainly was guilty (and received due punishment),
That perhaps that person is not innocent
Who entrusts the defence of his garden to a Donkey.

XII
The Wolf and the Crane

That wolves are greedy, everyone knows:
A wolf, while eating,
Never distinguishes the bones from the meat.
However, to one of them came misfortune:
He almost choked on a bone.
A wolf cannot either moan or sigh;
The time had come for him to perish.
But fortunately a Crane happened to be near;
The Wolf with signs somehow caught her attention,
And asked her for her help.
The Crane thrust into the jaws of the Wolf her nose,
And with great difficulty from his throat pulled out the bone.
Then she asked the Wolf to give her a reward.
"You joke!" cried the crafty animal.
"Reward you for your labour? Oh, you ungrateful one!
Is it nothing that you have safely taken away
From my jaws your long nose and stupid head?
Well, friend, clear off,

And take care that in the future our paths
do not cross."

XIII
The Bee and the Flies

Two Flies prepared to go off to a foreign land,
And tried to persuade a Bee to go with them:
Some parrots had showered effusive praise
On distant lands;
And besides, they found it annoying
That, in their own homeland,
People welcomed them nowhere as guests
And, even more disgracefully
(What strange beings people were!),
Did not allow them to feed on the sweets
That were spread out on magnificent tables,
And instead devised bell-glasses for them.
In humble abodes too were there villains – spiders.
"Pleasant journey to you," the Bee said to them.
"But to me
It is pleasant even in my own country.
I have found love from everyone for my honeycombs –
From peasants right up to grandees.
But you fly whither you wish.
Everywhere you go you will find the same luck, my friends:
Not being useful, you will be welcome nowhere.
You are neither respected nor liked,
And even in another land
Only the spiders will be glad to see you.

He who labours with profit to his native land
Will not easily part from it;
But the one who lacks the ability to be useful
Will always find a foreign land enticing;
Not being a citizen, he believes he will be less contemptible,
And that no one there will find his idleness annoying.

XIV
The Ant

A certain Ant was gifted with strength so great
That it was unheard of even in ancient times;
He even (says his reliable biographer)
Was able to raise two big grains of barley!
For bravery too he was considered a wonder:
Whenever he caught sight of a worm
He would immediately bite into it,
And would even confront a spider alone.
Because of this, he enjoyed such fame in his anthill
That the only talk there was about him.
I consider too much praise as poison;
But this Ant was not of such belief;
He loved it, and conceitedly accepted it all,
And believed it all;
Indeed, his head was finally so stuffed with it
That he bethought himself of appearing in town,
In order to show off there his strength.
On a peasant's very biggest wagon of hay
He arrogantly crawled,
And drove very splendidly into town;

But, oh, what a blow for his pride!
He thought the whole market would come running to him,
As to a fire;
But about him nothing at all had been heard:
All the people there had their own concerns.
My Ant now, having taken a leaf, began to pull it:
Now he pressed it to himself, now he half-lifted it –
No one noticed him.
Finally, having grown tired of struggling,
He said with annoyance to the dog Barboss,
Who was lying near the master's cart:
"Is it not true, I must ask,
That in your town there are
People without sense and without eyes?
Can it be possible that no one notices me,
However much I strive for a whole hour?
At the place where I live it seems
The whole anthill knows me."
And in shame he set off home.

So thinks another fool,
That he astounds the universe;
But he amazes
Only his own anthill.

XV
The Shepherd and the Sea

A Shepherd lived near Neptune's realm:
On the seashore, the inhabitant of a comfortable hut,

He was the contented owner of a little flock,
And quietly led his life.
He knew not luxury, but then neither did he know grief,
And for a long time he was perhaps more satisfied
With his fate than many kings.
But, seeing time and again how, from the sea,
Ships carried mountains of treasure;
And how rich goods were unloaded
To fill bursting storehouses;
And how their owners prospered in splendour,
The Shepherd was lured into trade.
He sold off his flock and house, bought up a supply of goods,
Embarked on a ship – and set off to sea.
But his voyage was short;
Deception comes naturally to the sea,
And he soon experienced that deception:
The shore was only just out of sight when a storm arose;
The ship broke up, the goods went to the bottom,
And only with difficulty did he save himself.
Now again, thanks to the sea,
He became a Shepherd, only with this difference:
Whereas formerly he grazed his own sheep,
Now he grazed someone else's – for payment.
If the need arises, however great it may be,
What will one not achieve with patience and labour?
By eating frugally and drinking little,
He amassed money, and began to acquire sheep,
And became again a shepherd of his own flock.
And so, one day, sitting in clear weather
With his own flock by the seashore,
And seeing how calm was the surface of the water
(By then, the sea had calmed down)

And how smoothly vessels sailed on it to the pier,
He said: "My friend! You seek treasure again;
But if you wish for mine, you wish in vain.
Find another whom to deceive;
I have already honoured you once;
I shall see how you entice others,
But from me in the future you will get not a penny."

I would consider it unnecessary to explain this fable;
But how can I not here add
That it is better to grasp the certain
Than to pursue a delusive hope?
One finds a thousand who suffer from that hope,
To one who is not deceived by it;
And so for my part, whatever people may say,
I shall keep repeating my belief:
What the future holds – God alone knows;
But what I have now is at least mine.

XVI
The Peasant and the Snake

A Snake crawled into a Peasant's house and said:
"Neighbour! Let's start to live more amicably!
It is no longer necessary for you to be wary of me;
You see, I have become something else entirely:
This spring I changed my skin."
But the Snake did not convince the Peasant.
The Peasant grabbed the handle of an axe, saying:
"You may be in a new skin,

But your heart is still the same."
And he killed the Snake with a single blow.

When you give a reason for changing your nature,
Change how you will your appearance,
You will not save yourself by it,
And what happened to the Snake may happen to you.

XVII
The Fox and the Grapes

A hungry Fox climbed into a garden,
Where a cluster of grapes glowed red.
The Fox's eyes widened, and her mouth watered.
The juicy bunches shone like rubies;
The only misfortune was that they hung too high,
And she knew not how to get them:
She had them with her eyes,
But not with her teeth.
Having tried a whole hour in vain,
She went away, saying with annoyance,
"Well, so what! At first sight they may look good,
But they are green – the berries are not ripe:
They will just leave a bitter taste in the mouth."

XVIII
The Sheep and the Dogs

In a certain flock of Sheep,
So that wolves would be unable to worry them more,

It was agreed to increase the number of Dogs.
What happened? In the end the Dogs were so much multiplied
That the Sheep were indeed spared from the wolves.
But, as it happens, even Dogs have to eat:
At first they tore the wool off the Sheep;
Then they drew lots and skinned the Sheep.
Finally, only five or six Sheep in all remained,
And those the Dogs ate.

XIX

The Bear in a Net

Mishka the Bear
Was caught in a net.
Joke insensitively about death from afar if you wish,
But when death is near it is quite another thing.
My Bear did not want to die.
He would have been prepared to fight,
But he was entangled in the net,
And from all sides there came upon him
Spears, and guns, and dogs:
So he saw no point in trying to fight.
Now Mishka decided to triumph by his wits,
And said to the hunter: "My friend,
What am I guilty of before you?
Why do you wish to have my head?
Do you believe unfounded slanders about bears,
That they are evil? Oh, we are not at all like that!
All the neighbours for example can confirm
That, of all the beasts, only I alone
Cannot be accused

Of touching a dead person."
"That is true," the hunter replied to him.
"I praise such respect for the deceased;
But then, where you had the opportunity,
The living themselves did not escape from you unscathed.
So it would be better for you to eat the dead,
And leave the living in peace."

XX
The Ear

In a cornfield, battered by the weather, an Ear,
Seeing behind the glass in a greenhouse
A pampered flower growing in comfort and safety,
Whilst he lay open to the attack of midges,
And to storms, and heat and cold,
Said with annoyance to the owner:
"Why are you – you people – always so unfair,
When something that is able to please your eye or palate
Is showered with care and attention;
Whereas what is useful to you suffers neglect?
Is not your main revenue from the cornfield?
But look how you neglect it.
Since the day you threw seeds here in the earth,
Have you protected us under glass from bad weather?
Did you arrange to weed or warm us,
And did you come to water us in a drought?
No: we were left to grow entirely by chance,
Whereas your flowers,
Which neither feed nor enrich you,
Are not, like us, thrown here on the field,

But grow behind glass in shelter, care and plenty.
If you cared as much about us,
Surely next year
You would harvest a hundred times as much,
And a caravan could set out with corn for the capital.
Think it over, and build for us a big hothouse."
"My friend," the owner replied,
"I see you do not notice my work.
Believe me, my main concern is about you.
If you only knew what labour it cost me,
To clear the forest and fertilise the ground for you:
There is really no end to my work.
But there is no use in talking about that now:
I have neither the time nor the inclination.
You yourself ask of the skies for rain and warmth,
And if I were to follow your advice
I would be left without flowers, and without bread."

Thus, often a good villager,
Simple soldier or citizen,
Comparing his lot with another,
Will start to grumble;
But the same could be said to him
As was said to the Ear.

XXI
The Boy and the Worm

Do not hope to find good fortune through betrayal.
Even those who consider a traitor base

Do not think it a sin to flatter him in time of need.
But the traitor will always be the first to suffer.

A Worm asked a peasant to let him
Reside in his garden for the summer.
He promised to behave honestly there,
Not touching fruits, only gnawing leaves –
And only those which had already begun to fade.
The peasant thought: "Why not give him shelter?
It cannot be, that because of a Worm
The garden would be too crowded.
Let him live here.
Besides, it would not be a great loss
If he were to gnaw two or three leaves."
He gave permission, and the Worm crawled on to the tree;
Under a twig he found shelter from bad weather,
And lived without need, though not in luxury;
And about him nothing further was heard.
Meanwhile the sun warmed everything,
And ripened the fruit in the garden.
One apple, ripening on a branch,
Was especially juicy, and translucent, like amber;
For a long time a Boy had been captivated by that apple;
He had noticed it among thousands of others.
But it was impossible to reach.
The Boy did not dare to climb on the tree,
And had not the strength to shake it;
In a word, he knew not how to get the apple.
Who offered to help the boy get it? The Worm.
"Listen," he said, "I know for certain
That the owner has ordered the apples to be picked;

So this apple is likely to vanish.
However, I shall undertake to get it for you.
I ask only that you share it with me. Your share may be
Even ten times more than mine,
But to me a whole lifetime will be more than enough
To gnaw even a very small portion.
The condition was accepted: the boy agreed;
The worm crawled up the apple tree – and set to work;
In a minute he had gnawed through the stem.
But what did he receive as a reward?
As soon as the apple fell,
The Boy ate it, complete with seeds;
But when for his share the Worm crawled down,
The Boy flattened him under his heel.
And that was the end of both apple and Worm.

XXII
The Funeral

In Egypt in antiquity the custom was observed
That when they wanted to bury someone more splendidly,
Women were hired as mourners and sent to wail
behind the coffin.
So once, at the interment of a distinguished man,
A crowd of these mourners were accompanying the deceased
To his repose, after a short life, in the house of eternal rest.
Here a wanderer, thinking from the outpouring
of heartfelt grief
That all the mourners were relatives of the deceased, said:
"Tell me, would you not be glad,
If he were resurrected for you?

I am a magician; I am able to do this.
We carry with us such incantations,
As can immediately revive one deceased."
"Father!" they all cried. "Yes! make us happy, us poor ones!
Just one favour in addition shall we ask:
That in five days or so he would die again.
When he was alive he was of no use,
And it is unlikely that he will be in the future;
But if he dies
Then maybe they will again hire us to howl over him."

There are many rich men
Who are only useful after death.

XXIII
The Industrious Bear

Seeing a peasant who was crafting shaft-bows,
And selling them at a profit
(For shaft-bows take time and patience to make),
A Bear decided to live by the very same trade.
Crashing and banging resounded through the forest,
And his mischief was heard from afar.
Of hazel nut trees, birch groves and elm trees,
My Bear destroyed a countless number.
But still he could not acquire the skill.
So he went to the peasant to ask for advice,
And said: "Neighbour, what is the reason for this?
Though I was able to fell the trees,
I could not bend a single one into a shaft-bow.

Tell me, in what does the chief skill lie?"
"In that," replied the peasant,
"Which you do not at all possess:
In patience."

XXIV
The Writer and the Robber

In the bleak land of shades
There appeared in court before the judges
At one and the same time: a Robber
(He had been causing terror on the roads,
And was finally caught in a trap);
And a famous Writer of scurrilous tracts,
Who in his works had poured out subtle poison,
Instilling unbelief and spreading immorality.
Like a Siren he was sweet-voiced
And, like a Siren, he was dangerous.
In hell, the judicial process is quick:
There is no pointless delay:
In a moment the verdict was delivered.
On two forbidding iron chains
Were hung two big cast-iron pots:
In them were seated the guilty.
A pile of firewood was heaped under the Robber;
Megaera herself lit it,
And started such a terrible blaze
That the very stone began to crack in the vault of hell.
To the Writer, it seemed, the court was not so strict:
Under him at first the fire barely smouldered;
But then, the longer it burned, the fiercer it grew.

Ages elapsed, but the flames did not abate.
Under the Robber, the fire had long since died down:
But under the Writer, hour by hour, it became more ferocious.
Seeing no relief,
The Writer at last cried out amid the torment
That there was no justice at all in the gods;
That he had filled the world with glory,
And if he had written a little too freely,
Then for that he had already been punished enough;
And that he did not think himself more sinful than the Robber.
Now, before him, in all her beauty,
With hissing snakes in her hair,
And bloody scourges in her hands,
Appeared one of the three diabolical sisters.
"Wretched one!" she said.
"Do you blame Providence?
And do you dare to compare yourself to the Robber?
Compared to you, his guilt is as nothing,
For his cruelty and malice
Were harmful only while he lived;
But you… though your bones have long since rotted,
The sun will not once rise,
Except to light up new evils of your doing.
Not only does the poison of your creations not weaken,
But, spreading, century by century it grows more fierce.
Look…"
(Here she allowed him to behold the world),
"Look on all the evil deeds,
And on the misfortunes, of which you are guilty!
Look at the children, the shame of their families,
The despair of their fathers and mothers.

By whom were their hearts and minds poisoned? – by you.
Who, having mocked, like children's dreams,
Matrimony, authority, power,
Blaming them for all human miseries,
Strove to dissolve the bonds of society? – you.
Did you not through your teachings sing the praises of
unbelief?
Did you not clothe in alluring and delightful apparel
Evil passions and vices?
And so, drunk with your teachings,
Now all the land is full
Of killing and robbery, of dissension and revolt,
And is being led to perdition by you!
Of each tear and drop of blood in the land – you are guilty,
Yet you dared to try and save yourself by blaming the gods.
And how much evil is to be spawned in the world
By your books in the future?
So suffer: here is a measure of punishment
for your misdeeds!"
Thus spake the angry Megaera –
And slammed shut the lid on the cauldron.

XXV
The Lamb

How often have I heard such reasoning:
"As far as I am concerned, let others say what they want,
If only my conscience is clear."
No; care must still be taken,
If you wish not to diminish yourself in the eyes of others,
And to preserve your good reputation.

Young ladies! The most important thing for you to know
Is that your good name is the best of all embellishments,
And that this for you
Is more delicate than the flower of spring.
How often, though both your soul and conscience be clear,
Does one ill-advised glance or word, one careless step,
Give the opportunity for malignant gossip to wound you;
And then your reputation is no longer the same.
Perhaps you do not understand; perhaps you smile;
Perhaps I express myself badly; but your each and every step
You must think over in such a way
That there is nothing at all for malignant gossip to seize on.

Anna, my dear child!
For you and your friends
Have I thought up a fable. While still a child,
Learn it by heart; not today, but in the future
From it will you harvest fruit.
Listen to what happened to the Lamb.
Put away your doll;
My tale will be short.
A Lamb stupidly,
Having put on the skin of a wolf,
Went to walk in it around the flock:
The Lamb only wanted to show off;
But the dogs, having seen the silly young thing,
Thought that a wolf had come from the forest.
They leapt up, rushed to him, knocked him off his feet,
And before he could come to his senses
Almost tore him to shreds.
Fortunately the shepherds, seeing this, saved him.

But it is no joke to be on the end of dogs' teeth:
The poor Lamb, after such a fright,
With difficulty dragged himself back to the sheep-fold;
There he grew sickly, became weaker and weaker,
And suffered ceaselessly for the rest of his life.
But if the Lamb had been wiser,
He would have feared the consequences
Of resembling a wolf.

Book Seven

I
The Assembly of Mice

Some Mice once thought to make themselves famous
And, despite the cats,
To drive all the cooks and housekeepers mad;
And, moreover, to see that news of their doings was proclaimed
From the cellar to the loft.
For that purpose it was decided to convene a meeting,
In which only those were to be invited
Whose tail was as long as their body.
They believed one characteristic of mice to be
That those with a long tail are always cleverer than the others,
And in every way more accomplished.
Whether or not that is correct, we shall not now consider;
Besides, in the matter of intelligence, we ourselves often judge
On the basis of clothing or beard.
It is only necessary to know that, from general agreement,
Only those of long tail were to be admitted to the meeting;
Those others who unfortunately had no tail
Were to be barred from attending;
And this even if they had lost it in a fight,
Because such would be taken as a sign
Either of incompetence, or negligence;
And consideration had to be shown for those with a tail.
All the preliminaries were settled; the meeting was arranged.

As soon as night fell,
The proceedings were at last opened in the flour bin.
But the Mice had only just taken their places when,
Lo and behold, there appeared a rat without a tail.
Noticing this, a young mouse nudged an older one
And said: "By what dispensation
Does the tailless one sit here with us?
And what on earth has happened to our ruling?
Say something, so that she be quickly ejected.
You know how we dislike the tailless ones;
Besides, how could she be useful to us,
When she was unable even to preserve her own tail?
She will ruin not only us, but all those in the cellar."
"Silence!" said the older mouse in reply. "I know all that;
But this rat happens to be my cousin ."

II
The Miller

The dam at a mill sprang a leak:
The misfortune would not have been great
If action had been taken in time.
But there seemed no urgency; my Miller was unconcerned.
But the leak with every passing day grew bigger:
The water began to gush, as from a bucket.
"Hey, Miller, be sensible and do something!"
But the Miller said: "It's not serious;
I don't need a lot of water:
The mill has enough to last my life."
He did nothing,
But meanwhile the water flowed out, as from a tub.

And misfortune came at last:
The millstone stopped, the mill fell idle.
My Miller now noticed the loss of water: he sighed and grieved,
And thought of ways to save the water.
He went to the dam to inspect the leak,
And saw that hens had come to the river to drink.
"Worthless ones," he cried. "Crested fools!
Even without you I was losing water;
And you came here to drink it up completely."
And he killed them with a log.
How did that help?
Having neither hens nor water, he moved back to town.

I have sometimes seen
That there are such people
(And this little fable is meant as a present for them),
Who carelessly spend thousands on fripperies.
They think to help with the housekeeping
By saving the ends of candles,
And are glad to quarrel with people about that.
With such economy, is it surprising that the household
Falls very quickly into ruin?

III
The Cobblestone and the Diamond

A lost Diamond was lying on a path;
At last a merchant happened to find it;
And by that merchant
It was offered to the Tsar.

It was bought by the Tsar, mounted in gold,
And became an ornament of his crown.
Having learned about this, a Cobblestone grew discontented;
He was attracted by the brilliant fate of the Diamond
And, seeing a peasant, spoke to him thus:
"Please, fellow countryman,
Take me with you to the capital.
Why do I suffer here in the rain and the slush,
While our Diamond is so greatly honoured?
I do not understand why he is valued so highly.
For many years did he lie here next to me;
He is still the same stone, like a brother to me.
Do take me. Who knows? If I appear there
Then perhaps I too shall prove useful in some way."
The peasant lifted the Cobblestone on to his cart,
And brought him to the city.
Arriving in town, my Cobblestone believed
He would be placed at once next to the Diamond.
But his fate was entirely different:
He did indeed prove useful – but in the building of a road.

IV

The Prodigal and the Swallow

A certain fine fellow,
Having inherited a rich estate,
Set off zealously in wasteful extravagance,
And completely lost everything.
At last he was left with just a fur coat,
And that only because it was winter
And he needed protection from the frost.

But, seeing a Swallow,
My young man sold even the fur coat.
After all, and everyone surely knows this,
Swallows fly in to us at the approach of spring;
So he thought there was no need at all for a fur coat.
Why muffle up, when all of nature
Is expecting pleasant spring weather,
And frosts are being driven to northern climes?
The young man's reasoning was understandable;
He simply forgot the folk proverb:
One swallow does not make a spring.
And indeed: as if from nowhere, frost again set in.
Carts crunched through brittle snow,
From chimneys the smoke rose in slender columns,
And hoar-frost patterned the glass in window-panes.
The young man's eyes watered from the severe cold.
He saw the Swallow, the harbinger of warm days,
Who had frozen in the snow, and went straight to her.
Shivering, he was barely able to say through clenched teeth:
"Cursed one! You ruined yourself;
And, relying on you,
I am now without a fur coat at the worst time!"

V
The Little Roach

I may not be a prophet, but,
Seeing how a moth circles around a candle,
I almost always successfully prophecy
That my moth will burn its wings.
Here for you, dear friend, is a comparison and a lesson:

The Fables of Ivan Krylov

It is salutary for both children and grown-ups.
You may ask: is that all there is to the fable?
No, be patient: that was just an introduction;
The fable is coming.
But first I shall give the moral.
I see now fresh doubt in your eyes:
At first you feared it was too short,
Now you fear verbosity.
Nothing can be done, dear friend: have patience!
I myself fear the same.
But what can I do? I am now growing old:
Weather towards autumn is more rainy,
And people towards old age are more garrulous.
But so that I don't lose sight of the point,
Then listen: I have heard many times
That, considering small mistakes to be trifles,
People often try to find excuses for them, and say:
Why do you blame me for this? It is a prank;
But a prank may be the first step to destruction:
It becomes a habit, and then an obsession,
And allures us with great power into danger,
Allowing us in no way to come to our senses.
In order to show you more vividly
How dangerous can be overweening self-confidence,
Allow me to amuse myself a little with a fable;
Now, from under the pen, the fable by itself is coming,
And may usefully edify you.

Alongside some river,
I do not remember where,
Villains of the watery realm – fishermen –

Settled down to ply their trade.
In the water, near the steep bank,
Lived a playful little Roach.
She was nimble, and cunning besides;
And she was not by nature timid:
Around a fisherman's hook she would turn like a top,
And often, because of her, the fisherman would
curse his trade.
When, after waiting in expectation of success,
He pulls in his line, he does not take his eyes from the float;
Now, he thinks, a catch! His heart gives a jump;
He swings up the rod: behold – the hook is without a worm;
The little rascal, it seems, is laughing at the fisherman:
She takes the bait and avoids getting caught;
And, no matter what he does, cheats the fisherman.
"Listen," said another roach to her,
"It will turn out bad for you, sister!
Do you not have enough room here in the river,
That you always play around the fishing lines?
I fear that soon you will bid farewell to us.
The closer you are to the line, the closer also to disaster.
Today you escape, but tomorrow – what guarantee
do you have?"
But rational words to the stupid are like those to the deaf.
"Look here," said my Roach,
"Good lord, I am not short-sighted!
The fishermen are cunning, but your fears are groundless:
I see through their strategems.
Look, there you see a line! There is another!
Ah, here are more, more! Look, my dear,
How I shall fool those cunning people!"
And to the hooks she set off like an arrow;

She tugged at one, then another, and, ah! misfortune
befell her:
She was caught on a third.
Now, too late, the poor thing realised
That it would have been better to avoid danger at the start.

VI
The Peasant and the Snake

If you wish to be respected by people,
Choose with care your friends and acquaintances.

———————

A Peasant became friendly with a Snake.
It is well known that snakes are clever:
She so insinuated herself into the Peasant's confidence
That he swore by her loyalty, and could not praise her enough.
But from that time on, of all his former friends and relatives,
Not one so much as set foot in his house.
"For goodness sake," the Peasant complained,
"Why have you all forsaken me?
Does my wife not know how to entertain you?
Or is my welcome not warm enough?"
"No," cousin Matvei said to him in reply,
"We would be glad to visit you, neighbour;
It goes without saying
That nothing you have done has upset or saddened us;
But, judge for yourself, what pleasure is it if,
Sitting at your place, one always feels as if your friend,
Having crawled out, is going to bite someone?"

VII
The Pig Under the Oak

A Pig, under a hundred-year old Oak,
Stuffed herself to satiety with acorns and,
Having eaten her fill, had a good sleep under it;
Then, opening her eyes, she rose,
And began to dig with her snout under the roots of the Oak.
"Don't you know this damages the tree?"
A crow said to her from the Oak.
"If you uncover the roots, it may dry up."
"Let it dry up," said the Pig.
"That does not worry me at all:
I see little benefit in it;
Even if it were to die, I would not regret it in the least.
As long as there are acorns, I shall have something
to grow fat on."
"Ungrateful one!" the Oak said to her now.
"If you would raise your snout upwards
You would see that those acorns grow on me."

Thus does an ignoramus, in blindness,
Curse scholarship and learning,
And all scholarly achievements,
Not sensing that he savours the fruit of them.

VIII
The Spider and the Bee

I believe those talents to be worthless,
Which are of no benefit to the world,
Even though the world may sometimes admire them.

A merchant brought fabrics to a trade fair;
They were such goods as all have a need for.
The merchant could not have complained about trade:
Of buyers there was no end;
At the shop there was often a great throng of people.
Having seen how well the goods sold,
An envious Spider
Was attracted by the merchant's success;
He bethought himself of spinning for sale,
To compete with the merchant,
And decided to open a little shop by the window.
He laid the foundations, spun all through the night,
Exhibited his goods wonderfully,
And settled down, having puffed himself up conceitedly.
He stayed in his shop,
Thinking that as soon as day came
Buyers would be drawn to it.
Day indeed came. But what happened?
A broom swept away the prankster, together with his little shop.
My Spider was furious with anger.
"Well," he said, "I shall seek justice:
I shall ask all the world, whose spinning is finer:

The merchant's, or mine?"
"Yours: who dares to argue about that?"
Answered a Bee. "This has long been known;
But what good is there in it,
If it does not dress and does not warm?"

IX
The Fox and the Ass

"Where have you come from, wise head?"
A Fox, meeting an Ass, asked him.
"Only just now from the lion," said the Ass.
Where, my friend, has his strength gone?
He used to growl, so that the woods around would tremble.
I would run for my life,
As fast as I could, from that monster;
But now, in old age, sickly and decrepit,
Entirely without strength,
He rolls about in his cave like a log.
Would you believe that all the animals' former fear of him has vanished,
And that old scores are now being settled?
All who came near him took their revenge
In their own way:
Some with their teeth, some with horns…"
"But you, of course," the Fox interrupted,
"Did not dare to touch him?"
"What do you mean!" the Ass replied to her.
"What had I to be afraid of? Even I gave him a kick:
I wanted him to know an ass' hooves."

Thus, be you noble, strong,
Base souls dare not raise even a glance at you;
But only fall from the heights,
And expect from them insults and injuries.

X

The Fly and the Bee

In a garden, in spring, amid a light breeze,
Sitting on a slender stalk,
Swayed a Fly.
Seeing a Bee on a little flower, he haughtily said:
"How little acquainted you are with laziness,
To labour the whole day from morn till night.
In your place I would become ill in a day.
Consider, for example,
My really so blissful life.
My activities consist only
Of flying around balls, around guests;
And it is not a boast to say that in town are familiar to me
All the houses of grandees and the rich.
If you could see how I feast there,
When there might be a wedding or a name day;
I am always among the first to arrive.
I eat from china plates laden with food,
And drink sweet wines from shining crystal,
And before all the guests
I take what I like of delicious sweets;
Besides that, favouring the weaker sex,
Around young beauties I circle,

                 And sit to rest
        On a rosy cheek or a snow-white neck."
          "I know all that," replied the Bee.
             "But still, the rumour reaches me
                That you are not dear to anyone,
And that at feasts they only grimace when they see you.
     Often, even, when you show yourself in a house,
            They chase you away, and shame you."
    "Of course," the Fly said, "they chase me. So what?
When they chase me out one window, I fly in another."

XI
The Snake and the Lamb

            A Snake was lying under a log;
              She was angry at all the world;
        She had no other feeling but to be angry:
             She had been created thus by nature.
  A Lamb in the vicinity was gambolling and skipping;
           He was not thinking at all about the Snake.
      Now, slithering out, she thrust her sting into him:
             In the poor thing's eyes the sky went black;
            He felt his blood burning from the poison.
         "What did I do to you?" he asked the Snake.
              "Who knows?" the Snake hissed to him.
"Perhaps you came here with the idea of crushing me.
              I am punishing you as a precaution."
       "Oh, no, I did not!" replied the Lamb, and parted
                             with life.

In whom the heart is so created
That it feels neither friendship nor love,
And feels only hatred for everyone,
That one believes everyone to be a villain.

XII
The Cauldron and the Pot

A clay Pot became great friends with a Cauldron.
Though a Cauldron is by nature much grander,
What does that matter, where friendship is concerned?
The Cauldron stood four-square behind his friend,
While the Pot was just as loyal to the Cauldron:
In no way could they be one without the other:
From morn till night they were inseparable:
If, by the fire, they were separated, they grew bored.
In a word, they went everywhere together,
Even when being put on, and taken off the hearth.
Now the Cauldron bethought himself of travelling the world,
And invited his friend to go with him.
Our Pot in no way wished to be separated from the Cauldron,
And so sat together with him on one cart.
The friends set off along a bumpy road,
Jostling each other in the cart.
Where there were hills, ruts, potholes –
These to the Cauldron were trifles; but pots are by nature weak:
Each jolt to the Pot was a serious blow.
However, he did not think of going back:
The clay Pot was only glad
That he had become such friends with the cast-iron Cauldron.
How far was their wandering, I do not know.

But about this I am reliably informed:
The Cauldron returned home whole from the trip,
While of the Pot there remained only broken pieces
of crockery.

Reader, behind this fable is the simplest idea:
That equality in love and friendship is a necessity.

XIII
The Wild Goats

A shepherd in winter found some wild Goats in a cave;
In his joy he thanked the gods through his tears.
"It is wonderful," he said. "I do not now need treasure,
For my flock will be twice as big;
I shall not eat or sleep,
Until I have lured these dear little Goats to my place with food.
Then I shall live like a Polish landowner on my own estate,
Because flocks are to a shepherd as an estate
is to a landowner:
He regularly takes from them quit-rent;
He amasses butter and cheese;
Sometimes he also slaughters them;
He has only to provide them with food,
But a shepherd has a store of food for the winter!"
So he took food from his sheep to give to the wild Goats;
He nurtured them, pampered them;
He went to them a hundred times a day;
In every possible way he tried to win them over.
He gave less food to his own animals,

And had little time for them.
But it was easy to deal with his own flock:
He just threw them from time to time a little wisp of hay,
And if they complained, gave them a poke,
So they bothered him less and less.
But here lay the misfortune: when spring came,
All the wild Goats ran off to the mountains:
Life lived away from the cliffs seemed sad to them.
His own flock grew sickly,
And one after the other almost all perished.
My shepherd became a beggar,
Though in winter he had been dreaming of riches.

Shepherd! To you now I say these words:
Why give your fodder in vain to wild Goats?
Would it not be better to care for your own?

XIV
The Nightingales

A certain fowler
In spring caught some Nightingales in a grove.
The birds were put in cages and began to sing,
Though they would rather have been flitting
through the woods.
When you sit in prison, do you really feel like singing?
But there was nothing to be done: they sang;
Some from grief, others from boredom.
Among them, one poor little Nightingale
Suffered torture more than the others:

He was separated from his mate.
Captivity was more irksome for him than it was
for the others.
From his cage he looked longingly at the field;
He pined day and night;
But he thought:
"One does not overcome trouble
with lamentation;
Calamity makes only a thoughtless one cry:
A clever one seeks a remedy,
So as to assuage grief in some way.
I think I know how to free myself of this misfortune:
Clearly we were not caught to be eaten;
I see that the master likes to listen to our singing;
So if I please him with my voice,
Perhaps in that way I shall earn for myself a reward,
And he will end my captivity."
Thus reasoned the Nightingale, and began to sing:
With songs he honoured the twilight,
And with songs he greeted the sunrise.
But what happened in the end?
In that way he only aggravated his unhappy fate.
Because for those birds who sang worse,
The master had long before opened the cages
and window,
And released them all to freedom;
But for my poor Nightingale,
The more pleasantly and tenderly he sang,
The more closely he was guarded.

XV
The Birch Broom

A great honour was bestowed on a dirty Broom:
No longer did he have to sweep the kitchen floors;
Now he was entrusted with the master's coats
(The servants clearly had been drunk).
The Broom set to work:
On the master's clothes and coats
He tireless beat, as if threshing rye.
Indeed his labour was great.
The misfortune lay only in that he himself was dirty.
So what benefit resulted from his labour?
The more he cleaned, the more stains appeared.

Much damage is usually done
When an ignoramus does not stick to his own business,
But undertakes to meddle in specialised work.

XVI
The Peasant and the Sheep

A Peasant summoned a Sheep to court,
To bring a criminal case against the animal.
The judge was a fox: in a minute the proceedings
were in full swing:
Questions were put to both the defendant and the plaintiff,
In order to elicit, point by point and without emotion,
What was the accusation, and what the evidence.

The Peasant said: "On such and such a date,
In the morning, two of my hens were missing:
Of them, only bones and feathers remained;
But in the yard was seen a Sheep."
The Sheep for his part said he had been sleeping all night,
And for that called in witness the neighbours,
Who said they never knew him to be guilty of anything,
Neither of theft,
Nor of cheating;
Above all, they pointed out that he did not eat meat.
But here, word for word, was the sentence of the fox:
"In no way could the Sheep's explanations be accepted,
Since it is known that all rogues
Are skilful at hiding evidence;
According to testimony, it is clear that, on said night,
The Sheep did not absent himself from the hens' presence;
And hens are very tasty;
And the opportunity was there.
So I judge according to my conscience:
It was impossible that the Sheep could have restrained himself,
And not eaten the hens;
In consequence of that I order that the Sheep be executed,
And the meat given to the judge, and the skin to the plaintiff."

XVII
The Miser

A certain house-sprite was guarding a trunk of rich treasure,
Buried under ground, when suddenly to him the order came
From the demonic leader,
To fly for many years to the far end of the world;

And his position was such that, whether happy or sad,
He had to obey the command.
My house-sprite was greatly perplexed:
How, without him, could the treasure be protected?
To whom could he give it for safe-keeping?
Big expenditure would be necessary
To engage a custodian, build a storeroom;
But if left thus, the treasure might disappear.
One could not guarantee that, if left for even
twenty-four hours,
It would not be dug up and stolen:
People's sense of smell for the scent of money is keen.
He took time, gave thought – and finally devised a plan.
His master was a Miser and a skinflint;
The spirit took the treasure and went to him,
Saying: "Dear master!
I must leave home to travel to distant lands;
But I have always been happy with you;
So, on parting, as a sign of friendship,
Do not refuse to take my treasure!
Drink, eat and enjoy yourself,
And spend it without fear!
But when you die,
Then I alone shall be your heir:
That is my only condition.
However, let fate prolong your life!"
Thus he spoke – and went off. Ten years passed, another ten.
Having met his obligations,
The house-sprite flew back
To the paternal home.
What did he see? Oh, rapture!
The Miser with a key in hand

Dead from hunger lying atop the trunk,
And all the money was safe.
Here the spirit reclaimed his treasure,
And was sincerely glad
That the guarding of it cost him not a single penny.

When a Miser possessing gold does not eat or drink,
Does he not guard the treasure for the house-sprite?

XVIII
The Grandee and the Poet

A Poet brought an action against a Grandee,
And asked Zeus for justice in the case.
Both were ordered to appear for a ruling.
They arrived: one was lean and emaciated,
Badly dressed and poorly shod;
The other was all in gold, and inflated with arrogance.
"Pity me, autocrat of Olympia!
Cloud harrier, thunderer!"
Cried the Poet. "Of what am I guilty before you,
That from youth I have suffered the persecution of evil fortune?
Neither a house nor possessions do I have,
And all my estate lies only in imagination,
While my rival, without having had to work,
And without intelligence, is, like your idol,
Surrounded by throngs of admirers in sumptuous chambers,
And from luxury and abundance has grown fat."
"But is it really nothing," Jupiter replied,
"That the sound of your lyre will reach to future generations,

Whereas, about him,
Not only great-grandsons, but grandsons will
remember nothing?
Did you yourself not choose fame as your destiny?
To him in life I gave the blessings of the world;
But believe me, if he had greater understanding,
And the ability to recognise his insignificance compared to you,
He would, more than you, grumble about his lot."

XIX
The Wolf and the Young Mouse

From a flock, a grey Wolf
Took away a sheep to a secluded spot in the woods:
Not, of course, for a visit:
The greedy beast skinned the poor sheep,
And devoured it,
So that the very bones crunched between his teeth.
But however greedy he was, he was unable to eat it all;
He left a store for supper and lay down nearby
To rest, and digest the rich dinner.
Now, a neighbour of his,
A little Mouse, was attracted by the smell of the feast.
Between mosses and hummocks he very quietly stole up,
Grabbed a piece of meat – and quickly ran off
To his home in a hollow.
Having seen the theft,
Our Wolf
Through the forest raised a howl.
"Help! Robbery!" he cried.
"Stop, thief! O, I am ruined: he has stolen my property!"

In town, I saw just such an incident:
A thief stole Klimich the Judge's worthless timepiece;
And he cried after the thief: help!

XX
Two Peasants

"Hello, cousin Faddei!" – "Hello, cousin Igor!"
"Well, friend, how are you getting on?"
"Oh, dear man, I see that you do not know about my misfortune!
God visited me: I burned my house to the ground,
And since then I have been a pauper."
"What happened? It sounds a bad business, my friend."
"Indeed. At Christmas we had a big party;
I went with a candle to give fodder to the horses:
To confess, my head was spinning round;
I somehow dropped the candle, and only just saved myself;
But the property and all my things burned down.
But how are you?" – "Oh, Faddei, it's a bad business!
With me, too, it seems God has been angry:
You see, I am crippled.
How I stayed alive, I consider, indeed, a miracle.
I – also at Christmas – went to the ice-house for beer,
And I also, to confess, had too much to drink:
My friends and I were half-drunk.
But so that, being drunk, I would not start a fire,
I blew out the candle,
And in the dark a demon pushed me down the stairs so hard
That it left me only half a man:

Since then, I have been a cripple."
"You have only yourselves to blame, friends,"
Old Stepan now said to them.
"To tell the truth, it is hardly surprising
That you burned down your house, and you are on crutches:
It is bad for a drunk to carry a candle,
And hardly better in the dark."

XXI
The Kitten and the Starling

At a certain house was a Starling,
A poor singer,
But on the other hand a most distinguished philosopher;
And he made friends with a Kitten.
The Kitten was already a handsome young animal,
Quiet, and courteous, and well behaved.
Now one day the Kitten failed to receive his fair share of food;
Hunger tormented the poor thing:
He wandered disconsolately, plagued by emptiness;
The tip of his tail was lightly twitching,
And he was plaintively meowing.
So the philosopher undertook to instruct the Kitten,
And said to him: "My friend, you are very naïve,
Voluntarily to suffer such hunger;
In a cage above your nose hangs a young goldfinch:
Will you not show that you are a true Kitten?"
"But my conscience…" – "How little you know of the world!
Believe me, that is utter nonsense,
And only the prejudice of weak souls;
For big minds it is just a silly joke!

In life, that one who is strong
Is free to do anything.
Here is evidence for you, and here are examples."
Now, presenting these in his own way,
He fully set out his philosophy.
To the Kitten, on an empty stomach, it was convincing,
So he pulled out and ate the young goldfinch.
But this morsel gave the Kitten a taste for birds,
Though he was unable to satisfy his hunger with it.
Then the philosopher delivered another lesson,
To which the Kitten listened with great attention.
"Thank you, dear friend," he said to the Starling:
"You have brought me to my senses."
And, breaking open the cage, he ate the teacher.

XXII
The Two Dogs

A faithful watch-dog,
Barboss,
Who worked diligently in his master's service,
Saw an old acquaintance,
Zhou-zhou, a curly-haired lap-dog,
On a soft, downy cushion at a window.
Being as fond of her as if she were a relation,
He nearly cried from emotion,
And beneath the window
Yelped, wagged his tail
And jumped.
"Well, then, Zhou-Zhoutka, how have you been
Since the master took you into the great house?

Surely you remember how in the yard we often starved.
What duties do you perform?"
"It would be a sin to complain about
my fate," replied Zhou-Zhou.
"My master thinks the world of me;
I live in ease and prosperity;
I eat and drink from silver bowls;
I gambol with the master; and, if I grow tired,
I lie about on the carpets and a soft sofa.
But how are you?" – "I," replied Barboss,
Lowering his tail and dejectedly hanging his head,
"Live as before: I suffer cold,
And hunger,
And, protecting the master's house,
I sleep here under the fence and get soaked in the rain;
And if I start to bark for no reason,
Then I take a beating too.
But how did you, Zhou-Zhou, fall into favour,
Being so weak and small,
While life for me is such a struggle?
What do you do?"
"What do I do? It's easy!" Zhou-Zhou replied teasingly.
"I sit up on my hind legs."

How many find good fortune
Only by sitting up on their hind legs.

XXIII
The Cat and the Nightingale

A Cat caught a Nightingale,
Dug her claws into the poor thing
And, gripping it tenderly, said:
"Little Nightingale, my dear!
I hear that everyone praises you for your voice,
And places you among the best singers.
My friend the fox tells me
That your voice is so pure and wonderful
That all shepherds and shepherdesses
Are mad about your singing.
I myself would very much like
To listen to you.
Don't tremble so, don't be stubborn, my friend;
Don't be afraid: I do not at all want to eat you.
Just sing something to me: I shall give you your freedom,
Shall release you to fly out through the groves and woods.
In love of music I am not inferior to you;
I often fall asleep purring to myself."
Meanwhile, my poor Nightingale
Was barely breathing in the Cat's claws.
"Well, what about it?" continued the Cat.
"Sing, little friend, if only a little."
But our singer could not sing, and just squeaked.
"So is it with this that you captivate the forest?"
The Cat asked mockingly.
"Where on earth is that purity and strength
About which all incessantly talk?
To me such a squeak would be boring even from my kittens.

No, I see you have no skill at all in singing;
It is all without a beginning, without an end!
So now we shall see how tasty you are."
And she ate the poor singer –
To the last morsel.

Can I whisper my thought more clearly into your ear?
A bad song results
When a Nightingale falls into the claws of a Cat.

XXIV
The Dancing Fish

Having in his domain
Not just woods, but waters,
A lion summoned the animals to a meeting:
Whom could he appoint as governor of the Fish?
As usually happens, it went to a vote –
And a fox was elected.
So the dear fox settled into the leadership role.
The fox noticeably began to put on weight.
She had a little peasant friend – like a close relative.
They two together had a good idea:
While from the shore the fox gave advice and supervised,
His companion caught Fish,
And shared them with him, as a true friend.
But clever tricks do not always have a happy outcome;
The lion grew suspicious due to rumours
That the scales of justice in his realm had become unbalanced.
Finding time,

He himself set off on a tour of inspection.
He walked along the shore. The peasant,
Having hooked some Fish, had made a little fire by the river,
And with his friend the fox was preparing to feast;
The poor Fish were jumping in the pan over the fire;
Each, seeing its approaching end, was flapping about,
Showing the peasant its gaping mouth.
"Who are you? What are you doing?" angrily asked the lion.
"Great sovereign!" replied the fox.
(The cunning fox always has a ready tongue.)
"Great Sovereign!
This, here, is my chief secretary,
Respected for his disinterestedness by all people.
But these crucians are only dwellers of the water.
We all came here,
Good Tsar, to celebrate your arrival."
"Well, what is the state of the river? Are my subjects happy?"
"Great sovereign, life for them here is not ordinary,
but a paradise;
If only your precious life be prolonged"
(The Fish meanwhile were jumping in the frying pan.)
"But why," asked the lion, "you tell me,
Do they flap so with their heads and tails?"
"Oh, wise lion," the fox replied,
"Having seen you, they dance with joy."
The Lion now, being unable any more to endure the obvious lie,
And deciding that the Fish should not have to dance
without music,
Forced the governor and secretary
To sing in his claws.

XXV
The Parishioner

There are people: only be a friend to them,
And they consider you the foremost genius and writer;
But then there are quite others,
For whom you may write as sweetly as you wish –
And not so as to expect their praises –
Yet in your words they are unable to sense any beauty.
Even if it annoys some a little,
Instead of a fable, I shall tell you a true story about this.

In a place of worship a preacher
(For eloquence, he was the heir of Plato)
Instructed parishioners in the virtuous life.
Sweet words flowed like honey from his mouth:
In them the pure truth, without art, like a golden chain,
Seemed to carry to the heavens all thoughts and feelings,
As he denounced the world, full of vanity.
The pastor of souls finished his exhortation;
But all were still entranced by him, and,
Transported to the heavens in heartfelt emotion,
Were oblivious to their flowing tears.
When from God's house the villagers came out,
One of the congregation said to another:
"What a wonderful gift!
What sweetness, passion!
How strongly he instils virtue into the hearts of the people!
But you, neighbour," he said, turning to a stranger,
"Obviously you have a callous nature.

Why do we not see tears from you?
Or did you not understand?"
"Well, how could I not understand?
But I have no reason to cry:
You see, I am not of this parish."

XXVI
The Brindled Sheep

A lion took a dislike to brindled Sheep.
It would have been easy for him simply to kill them off;
But this would have been unjust.
It was not in order to suppress his subjects,
But to deal fairly with them, that he wore the crown
in the woods.
But he had no tolerance for brindled Sheep!
How could he eliminate them, yet preserve his reputation?
And so he summoned to a meeting
The bear and the fox,
And revealed to them in confidence
That, each time he saw a brindled Sheep,
He suffered for the rest of the day with sore eyes,
And feared he might go completely blind.
How to avert such a calamity, he did not at all know.
"All-powerful lion!" said the bear, frowning.
"Why is there so much talk about this?
Order, without undue delay,
That one by one the Sheep be eliminated.
Who would miss them?"
The fox, seeing that the lion knit his brow,
Humbly said: "Oh king! Our good king!

You will probably not allow these poor creatures to be
driven away,
And will not shed innocent blood.
I take the liberty of offering different advice:
Give the command that they be assigned meadows,
Where for the ewes would be abundant fodder,
And where the lambs could skip and run;
And since we have a shortage of shepherds,
Command that the Sheep be tended by wolves.
I do not know, but somehow it seems to me,
That their species will disappear of its own accord.
Meanwhile, let them live in a state of bliss;
And whatever happens, you will not be involved."
The opinion of the fox gained influence in the council,
And so successfully was his plan implemented,
That in time not only brindled Sheep,
But plain Sheep as well, diminished in number.
But what did the animals say about this?
They said that the Lion was the soul of goodness,
And that the wolves were scoundrels.

XXVII
The Crow

If you do not wish to be thought ridiculous,
Keep the rank in which you were born.
Man of the common people! don't try to join the nobility:
If created a dwarf,
Then don't strive to be a giant,
But remember your size.

Having stuck peacock feathers into her tail,
A Crow conceitedly went to mix with peacocks.
She thought her relatives and friends
Would all stare at her, as at a wonder,
And believe that she was the equal of all peahens,
And that the time had come
For her to be an ornament of Juno's court.
What was the result of her arrogance?
That the peahens plucked out all her feathers,
So that when, headlong, she escaped from them,
Very few of her own feathers,
Not to mention the others, remained.
She tried to return to her own kind;
But they did not recognise her in the tormented Crow:
She had been completely plucked;
And her adventure finished thus,
That she was shunned by the other crows,
And yet was not accepted by the peahens.

I shall illustrate this fable for you by a true story.
The thought occurred to Matryona, a merchant's daughter,
To enter a distinguished family.
Her dowry for it was half-a-million,
So she was given in marriage to a baron.
What came of it? She was reproached by her new family
With having been born a petty bourgeois,
And by her own family for wanting to mix with nobles;
And so my Matryona proved to be
Neither a peahen, nor a crow.

Book Eight

I
The Aged Lion

A mighty Lion, terror of the woods,
Was stricken by old age, and had lost the will to live:
There was no strength in the claws; and none of those sharp teeth left
With which he was wont to inspire terror in his enemies.
His weak legs could barely drag him along.
But what was most painful of all –
Not only was he now not frightening to the animals,
But all, for old offenses, took vengeance,
Vying with one another to inflict insults on him:
Now a proud horse would kick him with a strong hoof,
Now a wolf would tear him with its teeth;
And then an ox would butt him with its sharp horns.
The poor Lion, in grief so great,
His spirit having been broken,
Endured everything and awaited his sad demise,
Only lamenting his fate
With a muffled and languid roar.
Suddenly he saw coming towards him an ass,
Tensing its chest and preparing to kick him,
And only looking for the place where it would be most painful.
"Oh gods!" wailed the Lion with a groan.
"So as not to be reduced to this shame,
Send quickly the end to me!

However hard my death –
It would still be easier than to suffer insults from an ass."

II
The Lion, the Chamois and the Fox

A Lion through the wilds was pursuing a Chamois;
He was gradually overtaking her,
And with a greedy look was already devouring
The rich and certain dinner which she promised.
To escape, it seemed, was for her in no way possible:
A ravine cut across the road ahead;
But the delicate Chamois exerted all her strength
And, like an arrow from a bow,
Leapt over the abyss,
And stood on a rocky crag on the other side.
The Lion stopped.
Now a friend of his happened to be nearby:
This friend was – a Fox.
"How," she said, "with your swiftness and strength,
Is it possible that you yield to a puny Chamois?
Only have the desire, and you may achieve miracles:
Though the ravine is wide, if you wish,
Then, probably, you will be able to jump over it.
So believe in my friendship and sincerity:
I would not risk ending your days,
If I did not know
Your strength and agility."
At this, the Lion's blood boiled up and was sent racing;
He threw himself with all his strength;
But he was not able to jump over the ravine:

Headlong he fell down, and died.
But what about his warm-hearted friend?
She very carefully descended the slope
And, seeing that flattery and kind deeds
Were by the Lion no longer needed,
She safely and freely
Began to celebrate the funeral repast of her friend,
And in a month had gnawed him to the bones.

III

The Peasant and the Horse

A Peasant was sowing oats;
Seeing this, a young Horse,
Muttering to himself, reasoned thus:
"Why has he brought such a lot of oats hither?
Look, they say that people are cleverer than us:
But what could be stupider or more ridiculous
Than to dig up the whole field,
Only so as afterwards pointlessly
To spread oats on it?
He should have fed it bit by bit to me, or to the bay;
If he had thought to scatter it to the hens,
It would have been more reasonable;
Even if he had stored it, that would have been just stinginess;
But to throw it to no purpose! No, this is simply foolishness."
But later, towards autumn, those oats were harvested,
And with them the Peasant fed that very Horse.

Reader! I suppose, no doubt,
You will disapprove of the Horse's reasoning.
But from ancient times, even to the present day,
Have people not in their ignorant blindness
In the same way impudently
Judged the will of Providence,
Not seeing in it either a purpose or a benefit?

IV
The Squirrel

A Squirrel worked in the service of a lion.
I do not know what she did, but the point is
That her service was pleasing to the lion:
And needless to say it is quite something to please a lion.
For her work she was promised a whole cartload of nuts.
Promised – but in the meantime the years flew by.
My little Squirrel quite often starved,
Though she forced herself to smile in the presence of the lion.
When she looked at the forest, here and there
She could see her friends, flitting through the treetops.
She could only blink her eyes,
While they went on cracking their nuts.
But our Squirrel, though just a few jumps away from the nut tree,
Saw that it was quite impossible to join them:
In the lion's service she was constantly needed.
And so the Squirrel finally grew old;
The lion grew tired of her: it was time for her to go.
He sent her into retirement,
And conscientiously dispatched the cart of nuts.
The nuts were sweeter than had ever been seen in the world;

All specially selected, nut by nut – wonderful!
Just one thing was wrong:
The Squirrel had long since lost her teeth.

V
The Pike

An accusation was made against a Pike in court,
That, because of her, life in a pond had vanished.
A cartload of evidence was collected,
And the guilty, as required,
Was brought to court in a big tub.
The members of the court gathered nearby:
They were grazing in a neighbouring meadow.
Nevertheless, their names were placed in the register.
These were: two donkeys,
Two old nags, and two or three goats.
For the oversight of due process,
A fox was appointed prosecutor.
There was a rumour among the people
That the Pike provided the fox with a supply of fish;
But despite this there was no partiality among the judges;
However it was, the Pike's wrongdoing
Could not be ignored this time.
So there was only one thing to do: the verdict had to be
To sentence the guilty to the most shameful execution
And, as an example to others, to hang her from a branch.
"Venerable judges!" the fox here began.
"To hang is not enough: I could devise an execution,
The like of which has not been seen here in a century.
In order that henceforth her fate may be a terror to rogues,

I recommend that she be drowned in the river."
"Wonderful!" cried the judges. They agreed unanimously,
And threw the Pike in the river.

VI
The Cuckoo and the Eagle

An Eagle bestowed on a Cuckoo the title of honorary
Nightingale.
The Cuckoo, in the new rank,
Settled down importantly on an aspen,
And set about displaying
His musical talent;
He looked, and saw all the other birds flying away;
Some laughed at him, while others abused him.
My Cuckoo was distressed,
And with a complaint about the birds flew off to the Eagle.
"For heaven's sake," he said, "by your command
I was given the title here in the woods of Nightingale;
But the other birds dare to laugh at my singing!"
"My friend!" The Eagle replied. "I am king, but I am not God.
I cannot save you from your humiliation.
I am able to appoint a Cuckoo honorary Nightingale,
But I cannot make a Nightingale of a Cuckoo.

VII
The Razor

Having met once with an acquaintance on the road,
I spent together with him the night in a lodging.

In the morning, barely had I opened my eyes,
When – what did I see? – my friend was already
in a state of alarm:
We had fallen asleep sharing a joke, without troubles,
But now he seemed a different man.
He was crying out, groaning, sighing.
"What is wrong with you?" I asked.
"My dear man!.. I hope you are not ill."
"Oh! It's nothing: I am shaving."
"What! Is that all?" Here I rose, and saw my prankster,
By the mirror, through his tears, grimacing as painfully
As if the skin were being torn from his face.
Having recognised finally the cause of his trouble, I said:
"How extraordinary. But you are tormenting yourself.
For goodness sake, look:
Surely you do not have a razor, but a meat cleaver;
You will not shave with that: you will only torture yourself."
"Oh, my friend, I agree;
The razor is very blunt.
How can I not know this? You see, I am really not so stupid;
But with a sharp one I am afraid to cut myself."
"My friend," I said, "may I assure you
That you will cut yourself more quickly with a blunt razor;
You would get a better shave with a sharp one,
If only you would learn how to use it."

I am willing to explain my story to you:
Are there not many people, though they be ashamed to
confess it,
Who fear those with a brain,
And more readily tolerate fools.

VIII
The Falcon and the Worm

Clinging to a branch at the summit of a tree,
A Worm was swaying in the wind.
Above the Worm a Falcon, floating through the air,
Joked and scoffed thus from the heights:
"What labour did you not expend, poor thing,
To crawl so high; and what benefit is it to you?
How do you manage to stay so high,
When you bend even with the branch, as the
weather commands?"
"It is easy for you to mock,"
Replied the Worm. "You fly high
Because your wings are strong and powerful;
But fate gave me different virtues:
I hold on here high up
Only because, fortunately, I am tenacious."

IX
The Poor Rich Man

"Well, is it worth being rich,
If you never either eat or drink well,
And only save up money?
And for what? We shall die, and surely give it all up.
We only torment and demean ourselves.
No, if riches would come to me by chance,
I would not spare a *rouble*, or even thousands,

In order to live splendidly and in luxury.
I would be known far and wide for my feasts;
I would even do good to others.
But the life of a stingy rich man is akin to torture."
Thus reasoned a Pauper with himself,
Lying on a bare bench in his vile little hovel,
When suddenly there climbed in to him through a crack –
Some might say a sorcerer, others, a demon;
From what follows, it will be clear
That the latter may be closer to the truth.
The creature appeared, and began thus: "You want to be rich;
I heard about that; I am glad to serve a friend.
Here is a small purse for you: in it is one gold coin, not more;
But if you take it out, another will appear.
So then, my friend,
It is now in your own power to grow rich.
Take the purse – and from it take out a coin as often as you like,
Until you are satisfied;
But just remember:
You are not free to spend a single one
Until you have thrown the purse in the river."
Thus he spoke – and left the Pauper with the purse.
The Pauper almost went mad with joy;
As soon as he had come to his senses, he got down to the purse.
What happened? He could hardly believe it was not a dream:
No sooner did he take out one coin,
Than another appeared.
"Oh!" my Pauper exclaimed.
"Only let my happiness last till morning!
Bit by bit I shall extract a pile of coins for myself,
So that by tomorrow I shall be rich –
And I shall start to live like a sybarite."

In the morning, however, he thought otherwise.
"It is true," he said, "I have now become rich;
And who – tell me – would not be glad of such a blessing?
But why should I not be twice as rich?
Could laziness possibly stop me
Spending at least another day over the purse?
Now I have enough for a house, for a carriage, for a *dacha*;
But if I can buy up a number of villages,
Would it not be stupid to lose the chance of that?
So I shall hold on to the miraculous purse:
I have decided: I shall fast
For one day more;
Surely there will still be enough time to enjoy life."
But what happened? A day passed, a week, a month, a year –
My Pauper had long before lost count of the gold coins;
Meanwhile, he hardly ate or drank;
As soon as another day dawned, he was again at the purse;
And when the day ended, according to his reckoning
He could still have done with more.
Whenever he resolved to take the purse to the river,
His heart would sink:
He would go to the river – and return again.
"How is it possible," he said, "to give up the purse,
When gold pours from it like a river, of its own accord?"
In time my Pauper went grey;
My Pauper lost weight;
Like his gold, his skin turned yellow.
No longer now did he see the point of luxury:
He grew weak and sickly; health and peace –
He lost both: but still with a trembling hand
From the purse he pulled out gold coins.
He pulled them out, and pulled them out… and how did it end?

On the bench, where he counted his riches,
On that same bench he died,
Counting his ninth million.

X
The Sword

The sharp blade of a damask steel Sabre
Was thrown into iron rubbish;
With the rest, it was carried away to market,
And sold there very cheaply to a peasant.
The peasant had some work to do:
He immediately found a use for the Sword.
He put a handle on the blade,
And with it in the forest began to strip bast for shoes,
While at home he unceremoniously used it to cut kindling.
Then he chopped branches for a wattle fence, and boughs for firewood;
Then he trimmed stakes for the kitchen garden.
Well, so not even a year passed
Before the smooth-edged blade grew jagged and rusty,
And was used by children at play.
One day a hedgehog, lying under a bench
In the shed where the Sword had been thrown,
Spoke to it thus:
"Tell me, what sort of life do you lead?
If all the fine talk about swords
Is not falsely spoken,
Are you not ashamed to chop kindling,
Or to trim stakes,
And, in the end, to be just a toy for children?"

"In the hands of a warrior," the Sword replied,
"I would be terrible to enemies; but here my gift is wasted;
So I am occupied around the house with only lowly work.
But can this be considered a humiliation?
No; it is really no shame to me: it is shame only to him
Who is not able to understand for what I am suited."

XI
The Merchant

"Come here, will you, Andrei my lad!
What's happened to you? Come here quickly,
And marvel at your uncle!
Run a business the way I do, and you'll be a success."
Thus in a shop spoke a Merchant to his nephew.
"You know the remains of the coarse-cut cloth,
Which for so long I had lying idle,
Because it was old, and damp, and starting to rot?
Well, I managed to pass it off as English worsted.
So you see, just now I exchanged it for a nice little
hundred *roubles*:
God sent a blockhead."
"All this, uncle, is so," replied his nephew,
"But I don't know who is the real blockhead;
Look carefully: you have been given a forged banknote."

———————

Everyone cheats! The Merchant cheated: no surprise there;
But if you look at the world
Beyond the shop –
You will see that there too the same rule holds;

Almost all have in everything a single thought:
Who can deceive whom more successfully,
And who can cheat whom more skilfully.

XII
The Guns and the Sails

Great hostility arose on a ship between the Guns
and the Sails.
The Guns, thrusting their muzzles out of the portholes,
Grumbled thus to the heavens:
"Oh, gods! When has it ever been known
For insignificant pieces of canvas
To have the audacity to compete with us in usefulness?
Just what do they do in all our demanding voyage?
As soon as the wind begins to blow
They arrogantly puff out their chests,
As if they are of some high rank,
And sail self-importantly on the ocean.
They only boast; but we – destroy in battles!
Is it not because of us that our ship reigns on the seas?
Do we not bring with ourselves everywhere death and fear?
No, we do not wish to live anymore with the Sails;
In all matters we shall manage by ourselves without them.
So blow, mighty Boreas,
And tear them quickly to shreds!"
Boreas obeyed – it puffed, then blew;
The sea frowned, and soon grew black;
The skies were covered with heavy storm-clouds;
The billows, like mountains, rose and fell;
Thunder deafened the hearing; lightning dazzled the eye.

Boreas roared, and tore the Sails in shreds and blew them away.
At last, the storm abated.
But what happened? The ship, without sails,
Became like a plaything of the winds and waves;
It drifted on the sea like a log.
The enemy, at the first encounter,
With all his guns on one side burst out with a terrible roar;
My ship, motionless, soon became a sieve,
And sank with the Cannons like a stone to the bottom.

Every country is strong
When all its parts are wisely ordered:
Weapons make it formidable to enemies,
While its civil powers are like the sails.

XIII
The Ass

A peasant had a Donkey,
Which behaved so submissively
That the peasant could not praise him enough;
And so that he would not get lost in the woods,
The peasant fastened on his neck a little bell;
My Donkey grew proud: his head began to swell,
and he put on airs
(He had heard, of course, about decorations),
And now he thought he had become a great personage.
But the outcome of his new rank was not as he expected
(This may serve as a lesson not only to Donkeys).
It has to be said, furthermore,

That the Donkey was not an honourable beast;
Before the bell was put on him he had a good life:
Whether he got into the rye, the oats or the kitchen garden,
He was able to eat his fill and come out unobtrusively.
Now everything went differently:
Wherever my noble creature butted in,
His new rank rang incessantly on his neck.
Everyone saw him: the master, with a cudgel,
Drove him away, now from the rye, then from the vegetable bed;
And sometimes a neighbour, hearing the bell in the oats,
Would poke the beast in the side with a stake.
Well, so, our poor Grandee
By autumn had faded away,
Until of him remained only skin and bones.

Even people in society
Have this trouble with rogues: while a rogue is of lowly rank,
That rogue is not so conspicuous;
But important rank on a rogue is like a bell;
Its sound is heard loud and from afar.

XIV
Miron

There lived in a town a rich man by name of Miron.
I put his name here not just to fill up the line;
No: it is good to know the names of such people.
About the rich man the neighbours on all sides gossiped
(And neighbours are almost always right),
Saying that he lived as if he had a million stowed away,

But never gave a *kopek* to a poor man.
Who does not want to acquire a good reputation?
In order to give the rumours about him a different turn,
My Miron let it be known to the people
That he would henceforth feed beggars on Saturdays;
And that whoever came to the gates
Would by no means find them locked.
"Alas!" everyone thought, "the poor devil will be ruined!"
Do not fear: the miser had it all planned.
On Saturday, from chains, he released vicious dogs;
And not only could the beggars neither eat nor drink,
It was a blessing if they could escape unharmed from the yard.
Meanwhile Miron almost entered into the company
of the saints.
All said: "One cannot admire Miron sufficiently;
It's only a pity that he keeps such vicious dogs,
And that it is so hard to get to him:
Otherwise he would be glad to share his last morsel."

―――――――――

I used to see very often
How access to great houses is difficult;
But it is always the dogs who are guilty –
Mirons themselves don't get involved.

XV
The Peasant and the Fox

A Fox once said to a Peasant:
"Tell me, my dear friend,
How did the horse so earn your friendship

As to be always in your company?
She lives in contentment; you lavish attention on her;
Whether on the road, or the field, you are always with her;
But surely, of all beasts,
She is quite the stupidest."
"Oh, my friend, the point is not about intelligence,"
The Peasant replied. "That is all irrelevant.
My reasons are different:
I need her only to convey me,
And to obey the whip."

XVI
The Dog and the Horse

Serving at a peasant's,
A Dog and a Horse once started to settle accounts.
"So," said the Dog Barboss, "big lady!
As far as I'm concerned they could drive you right off the farm.
No doubt it's a great thing to carry goods or plough,
But we don't hear anything about your other skills;
So how can you be my equal in anything?
Neither by day nor by night do I know rest:
By day I keep watch over the flock in the meadow,
And at night I guard the house."
"Of course," replied the Horse,
"You speak the truth;
However, if I did not plough,
There would be nothing here for you to guard."

XVII
The Eagle-Owl and the Ass

A blind Donkey lost his way in the woods.
He had set out on a long journey,
But by night the Madcap had gone so far astray
in a thicket
That he was unable to move either forwards or back.
Even a sighted one would have been unable to get out of
such trouble.
Fortunately an Eagle-Owl happened to be near,
And undertook to guide the Donkey.
Everyone knows that Owls are sharp-sighted at night:
Precipices, ditches, knolls, hillocks –
All these my Owl discerned as if it were day,
And by morning managed to lead the Donkey
to clear ground.
Well, how can one part with such a guide?
The Donkey now asked the Owl to remain with him.
He bethought himself of travelling with the Owl over
all the world.
My Owl, like a gentleman,
Settled down on the Donkey's back,
And they set off on the journey. But was it successful? No.
No sooner had the sun risen in the morning
Than in the Owl's eyes it became darker than night.
My Owl, however, was stubborn;
He advised the Donkey when to go straight, when to turn.
"Be careful!" he cried. "There is a puddle on the right."
But there was no puddle, and going to the left proved worse.

"Go more to the left, another step more to the left!"
And the Donkey, together with the Owl, went – bang! – into
a ravine.

XVIII
The Snake

A Snake asked Jupiter
To give her the voice of a nightingale.
"As it is," she said, "my life is hateful to me.
Wherever I appear,
All those who are weaker avoid me;
As for those who are stronger than I,
Please God – let me escape from them alive.
No, such a life I can no longer endure;
But if I could sing like a nightingale in the woods,
Then, arousing astonishment,
I would win love and, perhaps, respect,
And would become the focus of delight."
Jupiter granted the Snake's request;
She lost all trace of her vile hissing.
Then, having climbed up a tree, the Snake settled down
And began to sing like the wonderful nightingale.
A flock of birds flew from all around to sit next to her;
But, having seen the singer, they scattered like shot.
Who would be pleased by such a reception?
"Is my voice really that unpleasant to you?"
Asked the Snake in vexation.
"No," replied a starling. "It is sonorous and beautiful.
As it happens, you sing not worse than a nightingale;
But, I shall confess, our hearts began to tremble

When we saw your sting:
It is terrible for us to be with you.
So I say, though not to upset you:
We are glad to listen to your singing –
Just sing a little further away."

XIX
The Wolf and the Cat

A Wolf ran into a village from the forest,
Not to visit, but to save his life;
He was trembling in his skin:
Hunters and a pack of hounds were in pursuit.
The only trouble was,
All the gates were locked.
Then my Wolf saw on a fence
A Cat,
And begged: "Vasenka, my friend! Tell me quickly,
Who here is the kindest of the people,
Who will give me shelter from my wicked enemies?
You hear the bark of the dogs and the terrible sound of the horns!
They are surely behind me."
"Quickly," said Vaska, "ask Stepan: he is a most kind man."
"That is so; but I killed one of his sheep."
"Well, ask at Demyan's place."
"I fear that he too is angry with me:
I carried off his young goat."
"Well, run over there, where Trofim lives."
"To Trofim's? No, I am afraid to meet him too:
Since spring, he has threatened me because of the lamb."
"Well, it looks bad! But perhaps Klim will shelter you."

"Oh, Vasya, I killed his calf!"
"Well, my friend," said Vaska to the Wolf,
"I see you have earned the enmity of everyone
in the village.
What sort of sanctuary do you expect here?
No, in our men is not so little sense
That after their losses they will save you.
It is only right that you blame yourself:
As you have sown, so also must you reap."

XX

The Bream

In a pond in a landowner's garden,
In clear spring water,
Bream multiplied abundantly.
They swam playfully near the bank in shoals
As the golden days passed.
Then, suddenly, the landowner arranged
For some fifty pike to be let loose among them.
"For goodness sake!" a friend, hearing that, said to him,
"For goodness sake, what are you doing?
What good do you expect from the pike:
Surely not a scale of any of the Bream will be left.
Or do you not know how greedy pike are?"
"Do not waste your words,"
The landowner replied with a smile.
"I know all about that;
And I only wish to know,
What makes you think I am a lover of Bream?"

XXI
The Waterfall and the Spring

A foaming Waterfall, cascading from cliffs,
Haughtily said to a thermal Spring
(Which, though barely noticeable beneath the mountain,
Was renowned for its medicinal power):
"Is it not strange? You are so thin, so poor in water,
But you always have a multitude of visitors?
It is no wonder if many come to marvel at me;
But why do they come to you?"
"They come to be healed," quietly murmured the Spring.

XXII
The Lion

When a Lion became old and weak,
He grew tired of a hard bed:
It did not warm him, and was painful to his bones.
So he summoned his counsellors –
Shaggy-furred bears and wolves –
And said: "Friends! For one who is old,
My bed has become too hard:
So how would it be possible,
Without alienating either the rich or the poor,
To collect wool for me,
So that I do not have to sleep on bare stones?"
"Your Highness Lion!" replied the grandees,
"Who would begrudge you,

Not just his own wool, but his skin.
Do we lack here for shaggy animals?
Stags, hinds, chamois, goats –
They pay hardly any tribute;
Take their wool from them right now:
It will do them no harm;
On the contrary, they will feel lighter."
This very wise advice was immediately put into effect.
The Lion could not praise enough the cleverness of his friends;
But in what way were they clever?
In the way they took the other poor animals
And shaved them clean.
Though they themselves were twice as rich in wool,
They did not give up a single hair of their own;
On the contrary, each of them who were there
Profited from the same tax,
And provided himself with a mattress for the winter.

XXIII
Three Peasants

Three Peasants called in at a village to spend the night.
Here – in St. Petersburg – they earned their living by the
carrier's trade.
They had done some work, had had a good time,
And were now returning to their native home.
But as a peasant does not like to sleep on an empty stomach,
So our guests asked for dinner for themselves.
But what kind of delicacies are found in a village?
A bowl of thin cabbage soup was placed before them
on the table;

They were given bread, and what was left over of the *kasha*.
It would have been different in St. Petersburg –
But it is pointless to say that now;
Anything is better than going to bed hungry.
So the Peasants crossed themselves,
And sought comfort in the bowl.
Suddenly now one, the sharpest of them,
Seeing that there was too little for all three,
Thought of how to improve the matter
(If one cannot use force, one must be cunning).
"Lads," he said, "you know Foma,
Surely in the present conscription they will call him up."
"What conscription?" – "Well, there is a rumour
of war with China:
The Tsar has ordered that a tribute of tea be exacted
from the Chinese."
Now the other two began to discuss and argue
(Unfortunately, they were literate:
They read newspapers and, sometimes, military dispatches)
About how the war would go, and who would be
appointed commander.
They set off in conversation,
With conjecture, opinion and argument;
But that is just what their crafty friend wanted:
While they argued and discussed,
And deployed the troops,
He said not a word – but ate up all the cabbage soup and *kasha*.

One who knows nothing about a subject
Often talks about it more eagerly than others:
What is happening in India, the whys and the wherefores –

It is all so clear to him;
But have a good look:
The village burns down before his very eyes.

Book Nine

I
The Shepherd

Savva the Shepherd tended the landowner's sheep;
Suddenly one day his flock began to diminish.
Our young lad
Was sorrowful and grief-stricken:
He moaned to everyone and spread the news
That a terrible wolf had appeared,
And had taken to carrying off the sheep from the flock,
And killing them mercilessly.
"Well, it is not surprising," people said.
"What mercy can sheep expect from wolves?"
So they started to hunt for the wolf.
But how was Savva able to have in his oven,
Now cabbage soup with mutton, now a shoulder of lamb
with *kasha*?
(As a kitchen-boy, for his sins,
He was banished to the village to be a shepherd;
So his culinary tastes were similar to our own.)
They hunted for the wolf: everyone cursed him;
All the woods were searched – but there was no sign of a wolf.
Friends! Your labour was in vain: talk of the wolf was
just a rumour:
The one who ate the sheep was Savva.

II
The Squirrel

In a village, on a holiday, beneath a window
Of a landowner's mansion,
People were thronging.
They were gaping and marvelling at a Squirrel in a wheel.
Nearby from a birch tree a thrush was also marvelling at her:
She was running so fast that her paws
seemed to be flashing,
And her bushy tail billowing in the wind.
"Old fellow countrywoman," the thrush asked,
"Can you tell me what you are doing?"
"Oh, dear friend! I labour all the day:
I work as a messenger for an important gentleman;
You know, there is no time either to eat or drink,
Or even to take breath."
And the Squirrel began to run again in the wheel.
"Yes," said the thrush, flying off,
"It is clear to me that you are running –
But you remain at the same window."

If you look at another busybody,
You'll see him bustle about, rush around;
All marvel at him; he seems to work frantically;
But, like the Squirrel in the wheel,
He never seems to get anywhere.

III
The Mice

"Dear sister! Do you know, a disaster has occurred,"
A Mouse said to another Mouse on a ship.
"You know, a leak has been found: we have water below;
It nearly reached my nose."
(But the truth was – it only wet her paws.)
"And what is extraordinary, our captain
Either has a hangover, or is drunk.
As for the sailors – each is lazier than the other;
Well, in a word, there is no discipline at all.
I have just called out to everyone,
That our ship is going to the bottom.
And what happened? No one cared a rap.
It was as if I were spreading a false rumour.
But it is clear: one has only to look in the hold
To see that the ship will not last an hour.
Sister! Do we have to perish together with them?
Let's go, let's quickly throw ourselves off the ship:
Perhaps land is not far away!"
Here into the ocean my poor fools jumped,
And – drowned.
But our ship, piloted by a skilful hand,
Reached the pier safe and sound.

Now questions will be asked:
What about the captain, and the leak, and the sailors?
The leak was insignificant,
And was stopped in a minute;
All the rest – was untrue.

IV
The Fox

In winter, quite early, near a settlement,
A Fox was drinking from an ice-hole in a heavy frost.
Perhaps by mistake, or maybe it was fate (it doesn't matter),
Nevertheless – the Fox wetted the tip of her tail,
And it froze to the ice.
The mistake was slight; it would have been easy to put right:
She simply had to pull more strongly,
Even if it meant losing a tuft of fur;
And then, before people appeared,
Quickly to clear off home.
But how could she spoil her tail? And such a fluffy tail,
Spreading and golden!
No, it was better to wait – surely people were still asleep;
And meanwhile, perhaps, a thaw would set in,
And release her tail from the ice.
So she waited and waited, but her tail only froze harder.
She looked – day was breaking,
People were stirring, and voices were heard.
Now my poor Fox
Began to struggle from side to side;
But she was unable to tear herself free from the ice.
Luckily, a wolf came running.
"Dear friend! Cousin! Father!" cried the Fox.
"Save me! My end has surely come!"
So the wolf stopped –
And came to the rescue of the Fox.
His method was very simple:
He cleanly bit off her tail.

Then, without a tail, my Fool set off home,
Very glad that she had saved her skin.

It seems to me that the meaning of this fable is clear:
Do not, Fox, begrudge a tuft of hair,
If it means you keep your tail.

V
The Wolves and the Sheep

The Wolves gave the Sheep no peace at all,
To the point where finally
The other animals took steps
To come to the rescue of the Sheep.
To this end a Council was set up.
It is true, a big part in it was played by the Wolves,
But malicious rumours are surely not true about all Wolves:
It was even said that Wolves were often seen
Walking quite unthreateningly near the flock –
When they happened to be well-fed.
So why should Wolves not also be represented in the Council?
Though it was necessary to protect the Sheep,
This had to be done without discriminating against the Wolves.
So the meeting was convened in dense forest;
The animals deliberated, discussed, argued;
And finally devised a law.
Here it is, word for word:
"As soon as a Wolf near the flock starts to misbehave,
And begins to worry a Sheep,
Then in this case the Sheep has the right,

Without singling out any individual,
To seize any of them by the scruff of the neck,
And immediately take him to court,
Either in the neighbouring grove, or in the nearest forest."
There was nothing either to add to the law or take away from it.
But up to now I have noticed that,
Though they say even Wolves cannot escape justice,
Whether Sheep be defendants or plaintiffs,
The Wolves still go on
Carrying them off to the forest.

VI

The Peasant and the Dog

A Dog belonging to a Peasant, a very thrifty man,
Owner of a prosperous estate,
Was given the job of both guarding the property
And baking bread
And, in addition, of weeding and watering the seedlings.
"What nonsense he has invented," the reader might say.
"There is neither rhyme nor reason here.
Let the Dog guard the property;
But has it ever been known that dogs bake bread,
Or water seedlings?"
Reader! I would not be completely truthful if I said: "Yes."
But the point here is not about that,
Rather about this: that our Barboss undertook all three jobs,
And demanded wages for them all.
The arrangement was good for Barboss: what need had he for others?
One day the Master prepared to go to a trade fair.

He went, enjoyed himself – and came back.
But at home he discovered that things had not gone well:
He found there was neither bread, nor seedlings;
But above all, a thief had got into the property
And completely cleaned out the pantry.
The Peasant ranted and raved in fury,
And rained down abuse on Barboss.
But the Dog had prepared excuses for everything:
He had not been able to bake bread because of the seedlings;
And the seedlings failed because,
Guarding the estate, he was worn out.
And the reason he was unable to guard against thieves
Was that he had to bake bread.

VII
The Two Boys

"Senyusha, do you know,
Before they drive us to school again like sheep,
Let's go and pick chestnuts in the garden."
"No, Fedya, those chestnuts are not for us.
Surely you know how high the tree is:
Neither of us would be able to climb it;
In no way can we get those chestnuts."
"Well, my friend, I have an idea:
If one doesn't have strength, one must have brains.
I have thought of everything: be patient.
Just help me up on to the nearest bough;
And then we shall find a way
To eat our fill of chestnuts."
So the friends rushed with all haste to the tree,

And Senya helped his comrade to clamber up.
He strained, and panted, until bathed in sweat,
And at last helped Fedya to climb the tree.
Fedya struggled up to the high branches:
At the top he had the freedom of a mouse in a granary.
Not only could he not eat all the chestnuts he saw,
He could not even count them!
There would be enough for him, not just to eat,
But to share with his friend.
But what happened? Senya had little benefit from the exploit;
He, poor thing, only drooled at the bottom;
Fedyusha, at the top, ate the chestnuts,
And from the tree threw down the shells to his friend.

I have seen such Fedyas in life,
Whose friends
Help them to climb painstakingly up,
And afterwards are rewarded only with shells.

VIII
The Robber and the Carter

A Robber towards evening lay hiding in bushes
By the side of the road, hoping for spoils.
Like a hungry bear from its cave,
He was looking sullenly into the distance.
At last, a heavily-laden cart swept like a wave into view.
"Oh-ho!" my Robber whispered. "It must be
going with goods
To the trade fair: probably all heavy cloth, damask, brocade.

Away with sorrow – here will be enough to feed me:
My day today will not be wasted."
When the cart drew up the Robber shouted: "Stop!"
And fell upon the Carter with a cudgel;
But he found himself fighting a spirited opponent, not some oaf;
The Carter was a strong, well-built young man;
He met the villain in kind,
And defended his property with vigour.
And so my hero
Had to take the goods by force.
Long and hard, this time, was his fight.
The Robber lost about a dozen teeth,
And suffered a broken arm and knocked-out eye;
But he was left the victor:
The scoundrel killed the Carter:
Killed him – and went straight to the loot.
But what did he find? A cartload of empty sacks!

How often in life does no gain result
From wicked and criminal acts.

IX
The Lion and the Mouse

A Mouse humbly asked permission of a Lion
To set up home near him in a hollow.
This is what she said: "Though here, in the woods,
They say that you are mighty and renowned,
And that no one is your equal in strength,

And that a single roar of yours inspires fear in all,
Who will dare to predict the future?
Who knows who will have a need of whom?
However small I seem,
It may be that some day even I shall prove useful to you.
"You!" cried the Lion, "You pitiful creature!
For these impertinent words
You deserve death as a punishment.
Away! Go away, while you still live,
Or of you nothing will remain."
Here the poor Mouse, out of her mind with fear,
Set off with all haste – and was never seen again.
The Lion, however, paid for his pride:
Setting off to seek game for dinner,
He got caught in a snare.
His strength was of no use: in vain did he bellow and roar.
However hard he strained and struggled,
He still became the hunter's catch,
And was taken away in a cage to be exhibited.
Too late now did he remember about the poor Mouse,
That she would have been able to help him,
That with her teeth she would have gnawed through the net,
And that he had been destroyed by his pride.

Reader, loving truth,
I shall add to the fable, and not with my own words.
For good reason are people told:
Do not spit in the well:
It might prove useful if you are thirsty.

X
The Cuckoo and the Cock

"How resonantly and commandingly you sing, dear Cock!"
"And you, Cuckoo, my dear –
How delicately and mellifluously you sing:
We have not a singer like you in all the forest!"
"To you, my friend, I could listen a lifetime."
"And, my beauty, I swear,
That as soon as you fall silent I wait impatiently
For you to begin again…
From whence comes such a voice?
So pure, so tender and soaring!
Although in stature you are by nature slight,
In song you are a nightingale!"
"Thank you, friend; and as for you, I honestly believe
That you sing better than a bird of paradise,
And I am not alone in saying this."
Here a sparrow, who happened to be passing, said to them:
"Friends, though you may become hoarse,
praising each other,
The truth is that you both sing badly."

Why, not fearing to utter a lie,
Does the Cuckoo praise the Cock?
Because the Cock praises the Cuckoo.

XI
The Grandee

A certain Grandee in ancient times,
From a richly decorated bed,
Set off to the land where Pluto reigns.
To put it more simply – he died;
And so, as used to happen, he appeared in hell to be judged.
His interrogation began immediately:
"What did you do? Where were you born?"
"I was born in Persia, and held the rank of Satrap;
But since, while alive, I suffered poor health,
I did not myself administer the region,
But left all the business to a secretary."
"So what did you do?" – "I drank, ate and slept,
And signed everything that he presented."
"Send this man quickly to paradise!" said Ajax.
"What! Is that justice?" cried Mercury, forgetting all civility.
"Oh, brother!" replied Ajax.
"You don't understand the matter at all.
Don't you see? The deceased was a fool!
What if, with such power,
He had unfortunately meddled in official business?
Surely he would have destroyed the whole region,
And now, here, we would have had trouble beyond measure.
So the reason he is being sent to paradise
Is that he scrupulously avoided doing anything."

Yesterday I was in court, and saw there a judge:
Well, it really did seem that one day he would be in paradise.

Fables Not Entered in the Nine Books

I
The Bashful Gambler

I found myself once in rowdy company;
To be more precise – I happened to be at an inn.
There was not much of interest to see,
Though I did observe an interesting game.
One fine-looking young man among the players
Seemed more daring than the others.
He was the model of recklessness,
Placing his cards on the table and betting boldly.
Suddenly, after one hand, he lost everything:
He was ruined, and no one would give him credit.
When it came to swearing, my hero did not mince his words;
The blockhead raged,
And only managed to stay in the game by wagering
his *kaftan*.
An hour later, my hero was left in just a shirt,
Like a stump on a bare field.
Then a messenger came to him, saying:
"Your father is dying,
And wishes to say goodbye to you;
He ordered me to ask you to go to him."
"Tell him," said my Gambler,
"That the queen of diamonds has ruined me.
He himself may come to me:
It would not be embarrassing for him to do so.

But for me to go along the street without boots,
Without clothes, hat or stockings,
Would be terribly shameful."

II
The Luck of Gamblers

Yesterday I saw a friend in a carriage.
My friend is a pauper, so I was very much surprised
To see how rich he had grown.
Then he told me the whole truth, hiding nothing:
He said he had won enough at cards to buy an estate,
And that he placed card-playing higher than all the sciences.
But today my friend came upon me on foot.
"I suppose," I said, "you have already lost all that you won."
But he, like a philosopher, replied:
"You know, everything in the world turns like a wheel."

III
The Peacock and the Nightingale

An ignoramus in science, but in music a connoisseur,
Heard a Nightingale singing on a branch,
And wanted to have such a bird in a cage for himself.
Finding himself in town, he said:
"Though I did not see that bird, whose singing I so admired,
And do not know what kind it was,
Still, I wish to have one like it,
And here in the bird-sellers' market
Shall surely find many of its kind."

Filled with such a thought,
In order to select a bird at sight,
My gentleman arrived at the bird-sellers' row
With a stuffed purse but an empty head.
He saw a Peacock, and he saw a Nightingale,
And said to the merchant about the Peacock:
"I am certain that this is the charming singer I so wish to have.
Being so beautiful, it would be impossible for her
to sing badly.
Merchant, my friend! Tell me what this bird costs."
The merchant said to him in reply:
"This bird, sir, is not good at singing.
Take the Nightingale, sitting near the Peacock,
If you wish to have a good singer."
This amazed the ignorant gentleman not a little;
He feared the merchant wanted to cheat him;
He considered the wonderful Nightingale a worthless bird,
And thought:
That bird has such small feathers and body –
It is not possible that she is a singer.
So he bought the Peacock, and rejoiced in his purchase,
Expecting to take pleasure in its singing.
He rushed home,
And put the guest in a lattice-windowed room.
But the guest, as a reward for his choice,
Emitted screeches like a cat some ten times running,
Making it clear to the ignoramus from its screeching
That it was stupid to choose a voice according to feathers.
Similarly, like that gentleman,
Distinguishing with prejudice differences of intellect,
Often we number that one among fools
Whose clothes are not expensive, whose hair is not luxuriant,

Who is not adorned with rings and watches,
And who does not have trunks full of gold.

IV
The Unwelcome Guests

A rhymester
Had a house full of guests;
But his other-worldly mind
Was pre-occupied with prose and verse.
And being a little low in spirits,
He was irritated by the guests,
And asked me how to assuage his pain,
To get rid of them more quickly:
He thought he would go mad if they stayed longer,
But it was not possible to send them away
Without hurting their feelings.
However, he had only just started to read his ode,
When people suddenly began to leave,
And at the second verse he remained alone.

V
The Lion and the Hunter

To be strong is good, but to be clever is twice as good.
He who does not believe this
Will find here a clear example,
That strength without intelligence is a poor quality.
Having spread out a snare between trees,
A Hunter awaited his prey;

But somehow he blundered, and himself fell into
the clutches of a Lion.
"Die, contemptible creature!" roared the ferocious Lion,
Opening his jaws to receive the Hunter.
"We shall see what has happened to those strengths
By which you in your vanity
Boast to be lord of all animals, even the Lion!
When you are in my claws we shall see
Whether your strength is equal to your arrogance!"
"Not strength, but reason gives us superiority over you,"
Was the Man's reply to the Lion,
"And I dare to predict that,
With skill, I may overcome an obstacle
Which defeats even you with your strength."
"I am tired of listening to tales of your boasting."
"This is not a tale – I am able to prove it with action.
But if I lie,
Then afterwards you may still eat me.
Now observe: between those trees,
As a result of my labours,
You see a stretched-out net.
Which of us is better able to pass through it?
If you wish, I shall get through first;
And then we shall see if you in your turn, even
with your strength,
Can break through to the other side.
You see: this net is not a stone wall;
It sways with the slightest breeze;
But I say that with strength alone
You will hardly pass through it after me."
"Proceed, then," said the Lion haughtily,
Having examined the net with disdain.

"I shall be with you in an instant by a direct path."
Now my Hunter, not wasting unnecessary words,
Dived under the net and prepared to receive the Lion.
Like an arrow from a bow the Lion set off after him;
But the Lion had not thought to dive under the net:
He struck the net and could not break through;
He became entangled (thus did the Hunter settle the matter);
Art overcame strength,
And the poor Lion perished.

VI
The Feast

In a year of famine, in order to console his subjects,
A lion organised a rich feast.
Couriers and messengers were sent out to invite guests:
Beasts, both large and small.
At the summons they came from all points to gather at the lion's place.
How could one refuse such an invitation?
The feast would have been a good affair even in a year of plenty.
And so there arrived a marmot, a fox and a mole.
They were late by only an hour,
But found the guests already at the table.
Unfortunately, cousin-fox had had plenty to do at home;
The marmot had been grooming himself;
And the mole had lost his way.
However, none expected to go home hungry
And, seeing an empty place beside the lion,
All three went to squeeze through into it.
"Listen, friends!" the snow leopard said to them.

"That place is wide, but definitely not for you;
When the elephant comes, he will force you out;
Or worse: he will squash you one after the other.
Thus, if you wish not to go home hungry,
Then remain by the door:
You will have enough to eat – and for that you may thank God;
But the places at the front are not for you:
They are kept only for the large beasts;
Those of the small fry who do not wish to eat standing up
Must stay at home."